RUIN ME

THE SUMMER OF SECRETS: PART 1

CHRISTINA HART

RUIN ME

The Summer of Secrets: Part 1

Copyright © 2019 by Christina Hart

All rights reserved. No part of this book may be reproduced or transmitted in any form or by any means, electronic or mechanical, including photocopying, recording, or by any information storage and retrieval system, without permission in writing from the copyright owner.

This is a work of fiction. Names, characters, places, and incidents either are the product of the author's imagination or are used fictitiously, and any resemblances to any actual persons, living or dead, events, or locales is entirely coincidental.

Formatted by J.R. Rogue

1

JULY 4, 10:14PM

Kitty

The secrets I left on the shore,
they were yours.
And you didn't need them anymore.
They stopped mattering when
I stopped shattering over every truth they held.
They were little pearls in my palm
and I let them go,
watched them drift out to sea,
far away from me,
where they belong.
Did you know that once-pretty things can sink, too?

I PRETEND NOT to look for him in the crowd.

The cracks and booms go off around me as I convince myself I'm just observing the people in our small town.

Wait, it's not ours anymore. It's just his now. Because I left.

I watch the finale of the fireworks light up the night sky, crossing my arms to keep the breeze from infiltrating my bones. Being about a hundred pounds soaking wet doesn't help keep you warm. And living near the lake—*again*—doesn't help with the chill. It's always cooler near the water. And as much as I like to believe I was a mermaid in a past life, I can't say for sure that it's true.

This all feels too familiar. This searching for him. My heart is always searching for him. I close my eyes and wonder if he feels it. I will him to feel it. To feel *me*. But here I stand, alone, on the Fourth of July.

I glance around at the couples, keeping warm under blankets on the beach. I see the hand-holding, the kissing, the whispers of sweet nothings in each other's ears. I wonder how many of them are happy. I wonder if they are in love the way I have always been in love with him.

My eyes are still wandering, raking over the people I once knew, trying to find the one I knew best. People start clapping as the last and most brilliant fireworks go off back to back, before fading and disappearing to black. I breathe in, sigh, let it out. Whatever it is, I act like it's normal. My flannel isn't doing its job here. *Cheap shit.*

Coming here was a mistake. I don't know what I expected, why I expected any different. I turn and walk the opposite way everyone else is heading. It seems I'm always doing that. In this instance, I move closer to the water as the surrounding people flee to their cars. I sit near the edge—not close enough to get wet—and take my sandals off. Wrapping my flannel tighter around me, I stare out at the lake, giving up.

But, in the next moment—call it serendipity, call it fate, call it torture—I turn. A man, about his height, dressed like he'd be, in a white T-shirt and jeans, is walking away, slowly. I see the smoke trailing behind him. The muscular but not too muscular form. A hint of a bicep as he tosses his cigarette and stomps it out with his boot.

Pick it up. Pick it up.

He bends to pick the butt up off the ground. And I see, it's *him*.

I stare. For too long, I stare.

Turn around. Look at me.

He must feel my eyes on him. I wonder if he feels the passion, reaching him all the way from here. He double-takes. He goes to continue walking, but he stops. And he turns again. He squints, like he can't believe I'm here.

You didn't know? No one told you?

And he starts walking toward me. The slight smile he has aimed at me—it's accidental, I think, a reflex, from a million moments just like this—is almost sad, almost playful. I could never tell with him. My sisters would say I am oblivious. He would say I never paid attention to the signs that he loved me because I didn't want to accept them.

My heart starts pounding and I'm taken back. To the days when we were even younger than we are now. To the days when I was a virgin and he, my first everything that mattered.

To spring, and his first motorcycle.

I had on my favorite bubblegum pink cat sweatshirt. *Eleanor Katherine Bordeau.* My name never quite fit me. It was too sophisticated, too...normal. Everyone close to me called me Kitty. Including him. *Especially* him.

I pulled the hood up with the matching cat ears. He loved that thing, while simultaneously hating how obnoxious it was. My long hair flowed down my back in a braid. I had on the knock-off Timbaland look-a-likes we grabbed from WalMart, specifically so I could go ride with him. And light acid-washed jeans with holes all over the place.

We went everywhere that day. That's what it felt like. To the bank, to the store, to the movies, to dinner, to pay his rent. At some point, I think he was driving just to drive. I clung to his middle, stopping only to rub his shoulders and kiss his neck at red lights. He rubbed my leg on the highway, crept his hand back and found my crotch. I still don't know how he ever managed that with one hand on the bike, going ninety miles per hour.

But it turned me on. He knew that, used it as foreplay, building me up long before we'd get home.

We got back to his place, high on sunshine, on the breeze from the open road. The way the miles stretched on in front of us like we could ride forever like that, always with each other. Always touching, always at ease.

Always needing more.

I hopped off the bike first, like I always did. He followed close behind, a dog in heat.

"You have to stop touching me like that while we're speeding on the highway. You almost gave me an orgasm," I scolded.

He lifted my hood up and tugged on the ears, giving me that smirk that melted my insides. "Almost? I'll have to make up for that real quick."

I smiled and shook my head, teasing. "Oh n..."

Before I could get the word out, he picked me up, throwing me over his shoulder and heading toward the door.

He unlocked it with his free hand and carried me inside, spanking me once on the ass with just the right amount of firmness.

Once we reached his bedroom, he tossed me on the bed, climbing down my body, nipping at my clothing with his teeth.

"You gonna take these off or am I?" he asked.

"You," I chose, because of the way he always undid me. Slowly, deliberately, leaving me aching for more.

He started with my braid. Taking off the hairband, he unraveled it, unraveling me. He ran his hands through my hair as he kissed me, before moving to my neck. He gripped the sweatshirt, sliding it off with ease, then trailed kisses in between my breasts, down my stomach. He was squeezing, feeling, exploring. Appreciating every inch of me as he did every single time we made love.

He reached my jeans, finally, stopping once he undid the button, and sliding down the zipper. I was panting, begging. But him being him, he moved to my boots, untying the laces like he had all the time in the world. He took off my socks, then kissed my feet, massaging them, holding them.

He pulled my jeans off as I lifted my hips to help him, my head falling back against the pillow in anticipation. I could feel my panties being ruined by the desire coursing through me for him.

He moved up my legs then. Kissing my ankles, my calves, my thighs, making me squirm with the way he knew it tickled me *right there*.

He removed my panties last.

I had a black and white polka dot lacy thong on. He always ripped them. I never cared.

He rolled over, lifted me up so I was just above him. His favorite sight, he always said. My pussy, his pussy, it didn't matter. It was both of ours at that point. Only mine, and only his.

It was supposed to stay that way.

He reached around me, squeezing my ass with both hands as he pulled me down to him. I gripped the headboard, allowing him to take control, allowing myself the mind-bending pleasure he always gifted me.

Closing my eyes, I felt his lips first, tongue second. He licked me once, slowly, from my clit to the end of my slit, and back again.

"Joey." I moaned his name like he might stop, even though we both knew he wouldn't.

He licked in circles and rhythms that I never knew were possible before him. I never knew this could feel so fucking magical, until his mouth came along. He repeated the dance, making me come, gently at first, leaning into him as I moved my hips in rhythm with him and arched my back, tilting my head back in pure ecstasy. He moaned each time I came, every time, as though he was enjoying it more than I was.

With each twirl of his tongue, every agonizing stroke, he made me come harder, sucking my clit into his mouth like he was exorcising my orgasm from my body, and it worked. Every fucking time. I came hard in that moment, leaning forward, pushing myself into his mouth, his moan deepening with the intensity of my primal reaction to him.

He slowed then, giving me another two orgasms to come down from, before pulling me down onto him. I ripped his clothes off then.

First, his shirt.

Then, his pants.

I never had as much patience as he did. He always made me

want to fuck him like I'd die right then if I didn't get him inside me. And I did just that.

He was already hard, waiting. Wanting. And the sight of his desire just made me need him more. I kissed him, deeply, grabbing his hair as I slid on top of him, slowly, teasing my entrance on him so he could enter me easily. We always had to work for it in the beginning. His size and my size being slightly too large and too small to start. But once we fit, it was a blur of wild chemistry and sheer fucking need.

He stopped kissing me, leaned toward my ear and pulled my hair. "Purr for me, Kitty."

I smiled, both of us starting to laugh, before I shut him up by kissing him again.

But that was then, and I'm brought back to the now, as he's standing in front of me, looking the slightest bit lost, but mostly found. A ghost I'd only seen for the last two years in my mind, my heart. In vivid recollections like these.

"Joey," I say, breathless from the memory.

"Kitty," he says. "I've been looking for you."

The sudden urge to cry hits me then.

I've been looking for you, too.

2

JULY 4, 10:47PM

Joey

SHE WASN'T SUPPOSED to come back. After two years, I was almost starting to be okay without her presence. Without the sound of her laugh. I'd finally forgotten what her hair smelled like about six months ago. The scent remained on my pillows for almost two months after she left. Dirty, I know, but I refused to wash them at first. The pillowcases. At least with the faint keepsake, it almost felt like I could still hold her, in some way.

    I didn't know how many nights I could spend in that bed without her, without at least the reminder of the smell of her shampoo, her perfume. The sheets were a given. We'd fucked so hard in my bed, so often, that it just wasn't an option not to wash them.

    With her, I always wanted more, but never from anyone

else. No one else existed as long as she was around. And how could they? There was no one like Kitty Bordeau. At least not to me.

I knew it from the moment I saw her. A moment that plays back in my mind on loop.

I was at a bonfire, just shy of eighteen years old. The woman whose house I had just left was twenty-seven. I was pretty sure I smelled like her. Pussy has a distinct smell. As a man, you can recognize it in the air almost immediately. Even afterwards. And not in a bad way. I always loved it, at least if it was dripping for me. A subtle parting gift, thanking you for making them so fucking wet.

When I was first introduced to female parts, I couldn't get enough. I'd stick a finger or two in before slowly sliding out and putting my fingers in my mouth to see what that particular woman tasted like, savoring it. The women called me nasty, in a teasing way, but they made no attempt at hiding the fact that they loved it, and later, would get off on it.

I'd learned something in my early teenage years. Women wanted me. And not just the girls in high school. I mean real, full-blown women. Older women. Experienced women. Beautiful women. Women I sometimes didn't even know what to do with because no matter how much I satisfied them, they always wanted more.

And I gave it to them.

Ask and you shall receive. That was my motto back then. I didn't even have to search it out. As cocky as it sounds, they came to me. Being a Cherry Cove MC prospect promised that. The women flocked. And not just regular women. Gorgeous, sexy, damn near goddesses seemed to appear out of thin air most nights.

By the time my feet landed at that bonfire, I'd been with

more women than I could keep up with. It was every man's dream, but as a practically permanently aroused teenager, it was my reality.

The carnal desires, the momentary cravings, fulfilling them was fun. But amidst all the rough and kinky sex, the flings, the one-night stands with women who taught me—and blatantly told me—exactly how to touch them, there was something…missing.

The sex was great. I never complained.

But that night, at that bonfire, I saw Kitty and thought something for the first time in a long time.

I want to talk to that girl.

And that was it. I just wanted to talk to her. I didn't look at her and wonder what she'd look like without that cute little belly shirt on. I didn't view her as the potential for a little fun, much like the older women viewed me.

This beautiful stranger was sitting around the fire, on a tree stump, head thrown back and laughing hysterically at something. Her smile was the prettiest thing I'd ever seen. The effortless way she laughed and ran her hand through her dark brown hair. It was mesmerizing to me.

She had jean cut-off shorts on. My eyes traveled straight to her tan legs, the gorgeous bare thighs that were begging me to look. But I looked away, because I didn't want to miss her smile. That was where the prize was. I wanted to make her laugh like that. I wanted that smile aimed at me. I wanted it there *because* of me.

I'd seen enough beautiful naked female bodies to last me a lifetime at that point, even at such a young age. But that girl, nah. That *something* she had wouldn't allow me to walk away before talking to her. Everything in me wanted it. Needed it.

But working for it wasn't something I ever had to do

anymore. And in that moment, I wasn't sure how to approach her. What I would say.

Hi, your smile is the most perfect thing I've ever seen in my life.

No. Too desperate.

Hello, what is your name?

Too boring.

Wanna get out of here?

Too forward.

I lit a cigarette and looked at her for a few minutes more. She laughed again, and without realizing it, I started smiling. I didn't notice until she did.

One moment, she was laughing with her friends.

The next, that smile was aimed at me.

As soon as our eyes caught, her smile lessened in its natural vibrancy. I saw a shy one take its place. She tucked her hair behind her ear and took a sip of her Corona.

I knew right then, if she didn't look back over at me, I stood no chance with her.

But she swallowed her beer, and her eyes found me again. She looked…nervous. But she looked at me. On purpose this time. And that was all I needed.

I tossed my cigarette out on the ground and picked it up, putting the butt back in my pack before I started the walk over to her.

When I reached her, she was playing with her hair again, like she didn't know what to do with her hands.

"Is this seat taken?" I asked her.

She laughed. And this time, it was for me and only me. A small dream, that she just made happen.

"What seat? That's just grass," she said, still smiling.

I took off my leather cut and tossed the vest on the ground, which landed in a messy square. "It's a seat now," I said, sitting my ass on it before she could instruct otherwise.

She laughed again, shaking her head. "Oh, you're good."

During the brief pause, I looked at the bag resting by her feet, reading it before her eyes found mine again.

It said: *Bordeau Books: Where book boyfriends don't bite unless you want them to.*

I couldn't help but laugh. "What's the story behind that bag?" I asked her.

"Can't you read?" she replied, smiling.

I tried not to form the biggest grin and simply shrugged in response. "To a certain level, I'm sure. What's your name?"

"Why?" she asked. Her smile was gone.

"What do you mean why?"

"Why do you want to know my name?" she challenged.

"Why wouldn't I?" I said. "I saw that smile all the way from across the party."

She rolled her eyes. "Okay. You're *too* good." She stood up. "It was nice talking to you."

"Wait, where are you going?" I asked, confused.

"Home. To my sisters," she stated, as she was walking away.

Then it was my chance to stand. I started walking after her, trying to catch up with her. I wasn't used to chasing anyone. "Did I say something wrong?" I asked her. "I'm sorry, I…"

She turned then, placed a finger near my lips. "Stop," she said. "Those smooth lines of yours aren't gonna work on me. No matter how cute your little smirk is. I know who you are. This is a small town and I have older sisters," she hinted.

I looked down in response. *Fuck. What has she heard about me?*

"If you really want to know who I am, you're gonna have to try harder than that," she said.

In that moment, she gave me no choice but to look at her ass in those jean cut-off shorts as she walked away from me.

Now here we are, on the beach, the same beach that bonfire was at. Only, now I know her name. I know every curve of her body. Every nervous tic, every ticklish spot. But I still don't know every weakness of hers when it comes to me. Or if she even has any left. From the look on her face, I can't tell.

"Is this seat taken?" I ask her.

A smile it seems like she's trying to swallow starts to form.

I toss my leather motorcycle jacket on the sand and sit down next to her, stretching my legs out in front of me.

3

JULY 4, 10:52PM

Kitty

Unlike the old me,
I finally listened to what the tide told me.
I washed the ivory sands and your lies from my mind.
I willed myself to forgive myself,
my rib cage like a conch shell
that had been listening for echoes
of what I had mistaken for love.
But not even the land could find us.
The anchors I carried couldn't even hold us together.
This silent conch shell says there is no love left.
Our water graveyard has enough room for two.
I placed flowers down for the girl I used to be.
And none for you.

I LOOK at the motorcycle jacket on the ground he's sprawled out on. I look for the Cherry Cove MC patch. I look for the thing that tore us apart.

"You're still riding, I see," I say, a hint in my voice. The subtle reminder of what broke us, now breaking my voice.

He shakes his head. "It's just like you to assume the worst. I see not much has changed."

I snap my head toward him, making eye contact. "And it's just like you not to change."

His face softens. Turns into something I don't recognize.

Do I see pain there?

"I'm out, Kitty."

I start picking at the sand, the grains crumbling beneath my fingertips as I try to hold onto them. As I try to hold onto this past of ours. "What do you mean?"

Tell me you listened. Tell me you tried.

"I mean, I'm out," he says, looking me square in the face.

"What spurred that on?" I ask, looking away, unable to bear the regret in his eyes, not wanting him to see the sorrow in mine.

"You leaving."

He says it so simply. Like it won't affect me. Like it won't tear down my walls.

I look at him, the tears building despite my inward efforts. "That's what it took?" I ask, shaking my head. "I fucking hate that I was right."

I wipe my hands on my legs and stand up. Looking at him is too much for me. Seeing the love we once had, now swept away with every bad decision, every wrong choice. Every move made just one moment too late.

He stands, too. "Kitty, wait." He grabs my arm, gently. A

plea in his eyes. "I'm sorry. *You* left *me,* and I understand why. And I'm still fucking sorry about it."

I shrug my arm away from him. "I begged you to get out!" I scream at him. "For almost two years, I begged you!" The tears are coming now, but I wipe them away before they land. "Why did I have to leave for you to listen? Why didn't you love me enough to listen before you lost me?"

With a subtle shake of his head and fists balling at his sides, I watch him try to keep his composure. "I don't know. I was young. Stupid. Pressured. It wasn't that simple. You know that."

"Yeah, I know," I say, with a sarcastic laugh. "It was *much deeper than that.*" I repeat the words he often recited to me, back then, when I tried to steer him from his current life. From the shit he was getting himself involved in.

From the shit I didn't want to surround myself with.

I had lost my parents. Both of them, at once. In a horrific car crash. When I was eight. Their loss impacted me in more ways than I could even count today.

Their sudden departure taught me that sometimes, people leave you, even when they don't want to. Their deaths taught me that tragedies can come from love. That nothing is ever guaranteed.

That sometimes, you can kiss someone goodbye and have it be the very last time you get the chance, even when it's not by choice.

Abandonment, even when it's unintentional, leaves a scar. It leaves something in its wake that you cannot physically *show* to someone. It is only felt.

And it never goes away.

At least for me.

Joey knew this. He always knew this.

And still, he chose the path he wanted, for himself.

The violence, the drugs. The recklessness. All the things that came from being involved with a notorious motorcycle club. The beef with their rivals had gotten out of hand. The murders that had taken place. The small-town news, making international headlines. Their close ties with a much larger, much more infamous crew.

The danger he was in, daily.

The one percenter lifestyle he sucked me into, by default.

I remind myself now, he didn't care about me then. He didn't care about my safety. Even though he tried to convince me that he did.

And my dumb ass believed him. For too long, I believed him.

The club was always more important. It was always something I just *couldn't understand.*

And not for lack of trying. The oaths he swore. The bonds he built. The blood he spilled. None of it was meant for me. At least, that's what he always said.

At some point, I stopped believing him. At some point, I had to choose *me.*

Now, I look at him and wonder if I made the right choice. Even if it saved us both.

"It did go deeper than you knew," he says. "It was never about whether or not I loved you."

"You said there was only one way out," I remind him.

"I told you I'd die or die trying," he counters. "And I did. I lost everything. I gave it all up, willingly. Became a pariah in my own town. With my own people. For you."

I shake my head, begging more tears not to come. Silently praying he doesn't say whatever I think he might say. Hoping, inside, that whatever comes next doesn't kill me right where

I'm standing. Because this love I had for him—this love I *have* for him—it never went anywhere. It's still right here. Lingering in the space between us. In the spaces between the words we can't quite say to each other just yet.

"I did it for you. And only you," he says.

The sobs catch in my throat. A guttural cry I can't manage to form or squeeze out.

"Only, you weren't here to see it," he adds.

And with those seven words, I am gutted.

4

JULY 4, 11:11PM

Joey

"IT'S ELEVEN ELEVEN," I tell her, after the regret-fueled silence stretches on for too long. "Make a wish."

She grabs my hand and closes her eyes.

I look at her the entire time, rubbing the invisible message *I still love you* into the top of her hand with my thumb, like she might feel it. Like it might change things.

After a minute, she opens her eyes and looks at me, slipping her hand from mine to wipe her eyes.

"Hey, are you crying?" I ask her gently, knowing the answer.

She always does this when she cries. Tries to wipe the tears away before I notice them. The silent cries are usually worse, hiding away the things she won't tell me. Placing them in a box marked *Things Not Meant for Joey to Know*.

I always try to coax them out. Blow the dust off the things she's packed away. But it's her nature, to conceal. To hide. To run.

"No," she says, looking out at the lake.

"I didn't mean to upset you," I say to her profile.

"You never do," she says simply.

I nod and look down. "Well, you're definitely right about that."

She laughs and it's laced with sarcasm somehow. "Why are we even talking about this right now? Can't we just be two normal people and catch up like we haven't seen each other in two years? Can't we save the heavy shit for later?"

She looks at me, and there's something different in her face. I take the cue. The sign, that this conversation—*the heavy shit*—is over for now.

I let out a small laugh. "Guess we've never been that normal, huh?"

She laughs and this time it's genuine. "Nope."

"How are your sisters?" I ask her, changing the subject, leading her to the topic and people she cares most about in this world.

Immediately, her face softens. "They're good," she says, smiling. "Sophie's been spending her time teaching summer classes but they just ended, and Lucy, well, you should know. She's been here this whole time, running the bookstore by herself. I've been helping her out there, since I've been back. It's nice, us all being together again, you know? When it was just me and Sophie, it felt like a part of us was missing. You know my sisters are my world."

I nod. "I know. I'm glad they're both doing well. And you?"

"And me, what?" she asks.

"How are *you* doing?" I clarify.

She shrugs and it's noncommittal. "I'm okay, I guess. It took a while. But, I think I'm finally a little okay." She turns to face me. "And you?"

"And me, what?" I ask.

"How are *you* doing?" she mimics.

I swallow what I really want to say, unsure of how she'd react. "I'm all right," I say. "Still fixing up cars and bikes. I got out of the club but I could never abandon the passion." I stop to look at her, so she understands. "That lifestyle. It's really all I know."

She looks back at me, hard. There are concerns and accusations in her eyes, on the tip of her lips.

"What?" I ask her, softly.

"That lifestyle." She shakes her head. "So you got out, but you're still in." She stands up. "I should have known…"

I stand as well, reaching for her arm out of instinct. It seems I'm always trying to stop her from leaving. "Kitty, it's not like that. I've changed."

"How many times have you uttered those fucking words to me, Joey?" she asks me.

I look down. "Too many. But this time, I'm serious. This time, it's different."

"You got rid of the cut but you didn't get rid of the liar inside," she says.

Fuck. Acting like that didn't affect me, I stare into her eyes. "I'm done with all the shit that forced me to lie to you."

"Nothing forced you to lie to me," she says at the end of a frustrated sigh. "You chose to do it."

"I chose to protect you from it all," I tell her, because it's the truth. A truth she will never fully know or understand, for her own benefit and sanity. And also, because if she knew everything, she would never look at me the same. If she knew everything, she might never love me again.

She laughs. "Is that what you call it? You were *protecting* me? I have news for you, Joey. When you love someone, you don't lie to them. You shouldn't live a life you have to hide from them. Call them details, call them dangers, call them whatever you want. The fact of the matter is you were doing shit you shouldn't have been doing. And if you loved me, you would have stopped. To *protect* me, as you say. But you didn't. Not when I begged you. Not when I cried. Not when it was the only thing I wanted from this world."

I suck in a breath and wait for her to finish.

"You only stopped when you lost me because I *chose* to leave you. Always the same, having to learn the hard way. Always teetering on that edge of reckless abandon, wanting to see how much you can get away with. I guess me leaving had one good outcome, huh? It forced you to get your shit together. Not for my good, but for your own," Kitty tells me, like a knife to my jugular.

"Kitty…"

"No!" she says, starting to storm off and away from me. "You know what, fuck you."

I reach for her arm again to stop her and this time, I don't swallow the words I want to say. "You can hate me all you want, Kitty, but I still love you. I'll never stop loving you. No matter what you do or say."

She shrugs her arm out of my reach and gives me a long stare before she turns and walks away from me.

I let her go this time, knowing what she needs in this moment is space. And when she huffs and turns back around, I'm still standing in the same spot. Still watching her leave me.

She fights back the tears again but this time, a few escape.

"So much for saving the heavy shit for later," she says, with a forced laugh.

I shrug. "We were never normal, babe."

She starts walking again, only backward this time. "I'm not your babe anymore, Joey," she yells out to me.

And by her tone, I can't tell if she's being playful or serious. But I know her.

I know there's at least a small part of her that still loves me. And if it's the last fucking thing I do, I'll reach that part of her.

I know she expects some smartass remark from me. Something like…

We'll see about that or *You always will be*. But instead, I smile at her defiance. At the stubbornness inside her. Something I've always loved even though it always pissed me off at certain times. And I don't try to stop her.

Because it's not my goal right now to remind her why she left.

It's my goal to remind her why she stayed in the first place.

5

JULY 5, 12:24AM

Kitty

> *The wounds we soak, in salt,*
> *they burn just like we want them to.*
> *We're masochists, you know.*
> *We take all that **hurt** and roll it around in sugar*
> *until it comes out sweet.*
> *We're sadists, you know,*
> *trying to make the pain sound pretty.*
> *But the wounds we cloak,*
> *in sadness and solace,*
> *we never wanted them.*
> *We never asked for this.*

I CAME HOME EXPECTING my sisters to be here. I thought for sure I'd walk through the front door and hear their voices echoing gently off the walls, or maybe screaming at each other in bite size bits of fury, which seems more of the norm these days. But instead I'm alone in the kitchen, looking at the photos on the fridge. I briefly wonder if either of them, or both of them, are at the bookstore—*our* bookstore.

It still sounds so weird to me to say it's ours, and not our mother's. Bordeau Books.

The thing we're most known for in Cherry Cove. A little cursed town plopped down in the middle of going-nowheresville, surrounded by a lake. At least, that's how I think of it here.

Lucy, my older sister, might say otherwise. She clings to that store like it might bring our mother back, somehow. But Sophie, the oldest of the three of us, knows better. I think she always shared my notion on this small town, even if she didn't voice it.

Hence why she got a teaching job near the city and moved away at the first real chance she got.

And why I chose to go be with her, well, there were numerous reasons. Including—and mainly—Joey.

Being back here, in our home, brings back a flood of memories I'm not sure I was prepared for. I grab the one photo off the fridge, and a bottle of rum, and sit at the kitchen table.

I flip the photo over in my palm. *July fourth, two thousand and four.* I wipe the tear forming at the corner of my eye and take a swig directly from the bottle.

My parents' faces, smiling. A happy family, dark eyes and dark hair, looking back at me. I was the smallest, then. And still now. The baby. In the photo, I'm in the middle of my sisters. Sophie and Lucy are holding me in the air between them. Our parents are behind us, beaming with pride. Their three little girls carefree and laughing on the beach.

This small lake town has never been big enough for us. Our dreams, reaching beyond the lake, beyond the limits. I close my eyes and remember the crash, the phone call that confirmed our worst fears. Both our parents, gone. Killed by a drunk driver. Just like that.

One day, we were happy.

The next, we were not.

Sometimes life strangles you in this way. Rips those you love from you, from your life, from everything you've ever known. The violent struggle that ensues is almost enough to kill you, too. But you find that life is not that kind.

You will be spared, because mourning is something you'll be forced to endure. Even when you want it all to disappear.

You survive it because you have to. Because you have no choice.

And in my case, because you have two sisters to pull you through it.

Grief is a strange hole. It pulls you in, then spits you out.

Sophie and Lucy have always been my life vests. When we were tubing, when we were drowning in loss. When I couldn't fathom getting out of bed and going to school. When waking up seemed like a task I was not built for.

Depression was something that made a home in me as a child. It's lived there since, becoming a pulsing, breathing thing that vibrates inside me, even in my happy moments.

They took turns making my lunches. They went from sisters to mothers in a heartbeat, taking care of me. Making sure I grew up feeling as little of that void as possible. They filled it with their laughter, their hugs, their delicate influences that shaped me into who I am today.

And if they ever cried, it was never in front of me.

They never showed their sadness. Now, looking back, I

recognize that strength was solely for me. They allowed me to cry in their laps more nights than I could count.

They gave me the space to grieve, to question, to scream. And simultaneously, they gave me the freedom to blossom.

I grab the bottle of rum and walk outside. The wraparound porch on our charming two-story white home has always been a favorite spot of mine.

I guess some things never change.

I let my mind wander to where they are as I glance at the garage, looking to see if a light is on in the apartment above it. But it's dark, telling me Sophie isn't in there. I wonder where she is. If Lucy is at the bookstore, nose in a new release. I wonder if they miss me like I miss them.

Since Sophie and I came back, she and Lucy have been bickering. They think I'm too young to understand. But I understand resentment. I understand that we left Lucy to deal with everything, alone. To run the bookstore. To keep the lake house afloat.

Time is something you can't take back.

In the two years I was gone, I've grown, as I'm sure they have. Me, a little more. Physically. Mentally. I left a teenager and returned an adult.

Nineteen years old.

I wonder if they'll ever see me as an adult. Or if I'll always be the baby sister. *Their* baby. The impulsive and wild dreamer. The poet, chasing after romance and revolution. The one with the riot in her heart leading her in every direction.

I want to change our lives.

Maybe my pen can do that.

It's all I have these days. It's all I've had since I left Joey and this town behind.

6

JULY 10, 10:23PM

Kitty

The storm we never spoke of,
the lightning and fright,
the way it made me lose my way to you every night.
The thunder bellowing in my heart
was always echoing your name.
But the shelter from you, it never came.
I'm still stranded underneath you,
being pelted with rain.

I AWAKE to the sound of the rain hammering against the rooftop. The pitter patter, the light but persistent tapping. It reminds me of Joey.

Always trying to find a way in.

Always trying to break me down.

I want to shield myself from him. Force a barrier between us. A solid but gentle *no*.

But the gifts on my doorstep prove that he has other ideas.

I gather them in my hands, but I've run out of the energy to try to stop this. To try to stop him.

Did he ever give a shit what I wanted, anyway?

He either sent or delivered some of my favorite things. Three big bags of Reese's Cups. Three orchids, towering over my steps. All of which are different colors.

White.

Pink.

Purple.

Three bags of Fritos.

An envelope, with my name on it.

I open it up and find two tickets to *The Rocky Horror Picture Show*. A live reenactment. A show he was too cool to see back when he was in the club.

And there's a note inside.

Kitty,

The show is in nine days. Figured I'd send you nine different reasons to say yes. I'll be waiting for you at the entrance. Let's do that time warp thing you always ranted about.

Love,

Joey

My heart doesn't mean to, but it skips a beat. *Stupid fucking thing.*

I gather the candy, the card, the flowers. I can't believe he remembers all of this. The things that mean something to me.

The things that make me swoon, even if they are silly and small.

I imagine his smug smirk at watching my reaction to all this, and I ice over again. I freeze. The cold-stone bitch. The little brat. Even now, when he's trying to make me happy, I want to refuse him. I want to give him shit.

Because with him, there's always a catch.

There's always a reason for being disappointed right around the corner of being happy.

He always played it well.

He always reminded me that every good moment came with a price. Every smile came with a sadness. A heartbreak I couldn't learn to get over.

I take the tickets inside and shove the rest of the stuff onto the kitchen table. The flowers, I'm gentle with. Orchids always die under my watch. Even when I'm careful.

Maybe fragile things were never meant to be in my care.

Even him.

I gather the rest of the things I can carry to my room and I pretend they don't affect me. I pretend I can't smell him, here. In the card. In the note.

I pretend I can't feel him in the words.

The show is nine days from today.

I want to scream at him. That a show isn't going to solve things.

That this won't make things better.

But my heart. *My fucking heart.* It screams to try.

It's still screaming his name. Even after all this time.

I wish I knew what it was like to forget him.

He makes it impossible. Even when he doesn't try.

7

JULY 19, 8:37PM

Joey

I'M WAITING at the castle entrance. The old castle they've turned into a theater for plays. The show doesn't start until nine but I made sure I got here early.

She always hated when I was late. When I kept her waiting. There were too many nights to count.

The nights I'd get home from a run, hoping she was still up. The nights I'd find her fast asleep in my bed, still with all her clothes on from the day.

I hated myself those nights. The fact that she was waiting up for me, the fact that the club took me away from her the way it did. The responsibilities I had that I couldn't turn my back on. The drug runs. The rival conflict. The violence. The mayhem.

I put my cigarette out, pick up the butt and put it in my

pack, and wait, checking the time on my phone. Eight forty-three.

A brief thought crosses my mind that she might not show. And if she doesn't...

I can't allow my mind to go there. Kitty is the last thing in this world that matters to me. I never gave up on her. On us. I need her to know that.

I check the time on my phone again. Eight fifty-two.

Come on, Kitty.

The crowd outside of smokers, they make their way inside and I check my phone again. Eight fifty-eight.

It's two after nine when I get on my bike to leave.

It's four after nine when I rev it up.

It's five after nine when I hear her shout my name.

I turn around to see her and crack a smile for the first time all day. *This fucking girl.* She's got on some sparkly number with a matching glittery hat. Booty shorts. Fishnets. Wild makeup.

"Sorry I'm late," she says. "Putting together this Columbia costume was no simple feat."

"Where are your eyebrows?" I ask her, reaching out to touch her face.

She slaps my arm away in response and laughs. "If you ever watched the movie with me you'd understand."

"I'm here now," I say.

"Yeah, but you should've dressed like Frank-N-Furter," she says, grabbing my arm, a huge smile stuck on her painted face. "Let's go! We're gonna miss it!"

A COUPLE OF HOURS LATER, I'm traumatized. I've never seen so many half-naked men in makeup in one place and I have the rock song stuck in my head, but I'll never admit that to Kitty. *Hot patootie, bless my soul, fell in love with rock n' roll...*

I'm still humming it in my head when I turn to her. "So, let me get this straight," I say. "You wish I dressed like a transvestite?"

"From Transylvaniaaaaa," she sings as seductively as she can without being able to carry a note, dragging her finger down my chest to my jeans.

I stop her hand there. "Kitty, we're in public," I remind her, even though all I want to do is rip her ridiculous glittery clothes off right here in the parking lot.

"That never stopped you before," she whispers into my ear.

What started as joking suddenly feels serious, if the look in her eye is telling me anything.

And then I can't take it. Lipstick or not.

I grab her hips and pull her flush against me. "You think it'd stop me now? I thought you knew me better than that."

Even beneath all the makeup, I see her cheeks redden as she tilts her head back to look up at me. She's still about a foot shorter than I am.

"Do something about it then," she says.

My right hand moves to her ass cheek and squeezes before I hoist her in the air and wrap her legs around me.

My lips are on hers before she can rethink this. I kiss her slowly at first, holding her ass up with one hand while my other hand throws her hat off and pulls her hair. She lets out a small moan into my mouth and I feel myself growing hard in my jeans remembering what this sort of thing used to lead us to. The kiss deepens, and she grinds herself against me in a slow, torturous motion, making it clear that she, too, wants to give in to our old familiar urges.

"Let's go home," I say.

I watch her face contort as she stops to consider this, and instantly I want to take those words back. I didn't think before I spoke. *Is this it? The rethinking?*

"I'm sorry," I rush out. "I just...we're having such a good time. I don't want it to end yet."

"I don't know if it's a good idea. I don't even know what just got into me," she says, shaking her head like she might regret that kiss. "I shouldn't have come."

"I'm glad you did," I say.

"We can't do this shit, just jump from zero to a hundred," she says.

But we both know it's a lie. Because we can. We have done it many times over. The attraction between us is too strong, it's always been that way. This mixed with our kind of passion is undeniable, the end result nearly unpreventable.

"It doesn't have to lead to anything," I tell her. "Can we just spend a little more time together?"

She's out of breath as she looks at me, her hands needy as she moves them down my shoulders and arms.

"Fuck," she says. "Fine."

We walk to my bike and I hand her the helmet that I had fastened down to the rear pillion.

She takes it in her hand and runs her fingers over the personalized cat skull on the back. "You still have this?" she asks me.

I eye the slight crease on her forehead, trying to find my answer as to why she would think otherwise.

"You thought I wouldn't?" I reply, as I throw my leg over the bike and bring the kickstand up.

I turn the ignition key. As the spark hits the gas and causes the engine to come to life, I hope the same response is happening with her forgotten feelings for me.

I wonder if she still remembers feeling the vibration of this tired old motorcycle as she's perched on top of it, because I vividly remember how her thighs would tighten around me. And how she would purr into my ear that we needed to pull over soon.

She shakes her head and I see a wistful sorrow cross her face. But she puts the helmet on and gets on the bike, then puts her arms around me and says, "My sisters are gonna kill me."

8

JULY 19, 11:43PM

Kitty

Somewhere in your bed sheets,
that's where my heart bleeds.
I am a riptide,
you a reckless current.
In the depths we will crash.
In the shallow we shall drown.

"YOUR PLACE LOOKS THE SAME," I say as I enter the living room, my fingers grazing along the old coffee table he built.

The same gray couch—with the cigarette burn in the cushion from that night I couldn't keep my hands off him a moment longer—against the wall. An ashtray on the armrest of his side. Motorcycle magazines scattered across the table, and the plush gray blanket I bought him for his birthday three years ago, slung over the back of the sofa.

"You were the one thing that made it feel like a home," he says simply.

"Can you stop doing that?" I ask him. "Acting like I left because I wanted to."

He shrugs and I know this isn't a conversation either of us want to revisit.

"It's hard to just act like there wasn't a lapse in time," he says. "Because ultimately, you left. Regardless of the reasons, you did the one thing to me that you were always afraid I'd do to you."

I wince at his words. "That's not fair."

"But it's true."

There's a rumble in my chest. A wall, maybe, breaking down. He's got his hammer again and my heart, when it comes to him, is glass.

But tonight, I don't want to talk about that. I don't want to think about the fact that I left him, how he pushed me into doing so and gave me no other reasonable choice. I want to protect my decision, water it and let it live and grow into something I can hold onto to know that I made the right move. Even if it killed me inside.

And I certainly don't want to be having this discussion in glittery spandex shorts, a sequin top, and fishnets.

My mind flashes back to right before I left home tonight, as I tried to sneak out without my sisters noticing me.

Lucy's nose was in a book—as usual—and Sophie sat in the armchair.

Despite reading, Lucy looked up first and eyed my outfit with suspicion. "Where are you going?"

Sophie glanced up at me next. "Yeah, why are you dressed like Magenta?"

Lucy let out a frustrated sigh and closed her book. "She's clearly Columbia, Sophie. Come on." She pointed at me as if it wasn't obvious. "The hat is a dead giveaway."

"Okay, *Lucille*. I don't care which character she is." Sophie looked back at me. "Where are you going and who are you going with?"

"How could you possibly think I was Magenta? Do I look like a Transylvanian maid to you?" I joked.

"Eleanor Katherine Bordeau," Lucy started, her tone light but her eyes stern, "what don't you feel comfortable telling us?"

"What do you mean?" I had asked, grabbing a water bottle in the kitchen to avoid their eyes. I've always been a shit liar, and I couldn't look at them and avoid their questions convincingly.

But Lucy followed me into the kitchen. "Who are you going to meet?" she bluntly asked me, closing the fridge and meeting my gaze.

I swallowed then. "Um...just a few friends...from school..."

"From school?" she asked, doubt lacing her tone. "From *high school?*"

"Yeah. If you recall, we did grow up here. And what's with the third degree? How many times do I have to tell you, both of you," I said, making a point to raise my voice there and look at Sophie as well, "I'm not a kid anymore. I can make my own decisions, you know."

"And how many times do I have to tell you? You're nineteen, Kitty Kat," Sophie said. "Don't be in such a rush to grow up. Trust and believe, it's not all it's cracked up to be."

I rolled my eyes at them. "Well, I'm going. Don't wait up. I'll be home late."

I snuck out the door as fast as possible, knowing I couldn't dare tell them who I was really meeting up with. Just thinking about it, I can hear them now. The scolding. The insistence that he's bad for me. Bad in general. The reminder of how he broke me.

And here I am, in his living room, such a familiar place. We made so many memories on that couch alone.

I smile at the thought and look at him. He looks so damn cozy. So much like home, himself. I hate myself for wanting to touch him, despite everything. But that doesn't stop me. Hearts don't give a shit about logic. Hearts don't understand the definition of restraint.

So I walk the few feet between us and wrap my arms around him, reaching up on my tiptoes to snuggle against his neck. "I don't want to go over any of the bad stuff. Tonight, can we just, I don't know, enjoy each other?"

His arms snake around my waist and I hear his deep inhale, his warm breath against my neck moments later. "Let's not talk about what didn't work," he says. "Do you remember what always did?" His voice is raspy with need as his hands make their way to my ass.

Instantaneously, and too easily, he's pushed my buttons. Just like he always could. "Sir, you just ruined my panties."

He grips my hips and pulls me into him, grabbing my hair and tugging gently so my head tilts back. "The way I see it is you won't be needing them for a while."

My heartbeat increases as I look at him. "Oh yeah?" I ask coyly. "Why would that be?"

"Well, I haven't seen your body in two years. And I plan on

getting reacquainted, inch by beautiful inch," he says, lifting my arms up and removing my top.

But I can't take the slow descent. Not after all this time of missing his hands and mouth. "We don't have time for all that, Joey. I need you inside me. Now."

9

JULY 20, 12:05AM

Joey

"HAVE IT YOUR WAY TONIGHT, KITTY," I tell her, even though all I want to do right now is enjoy the taste of her on the tip of my tongue as I bring her closer and closer to ecstasy.

She pushes me against the wall in response, kissing me with a passion that leads me to believe that our lips meeting is the only sustenance she needs right now.

She hasn't kissed me like this more than a handful of times, most of which had occurred when she had a bit too much to drink and was feeling frisky. Her normally submissive persona has seemed to have been stripped away, now replaced by a ravenous woman with only one thing on her mind.

She grabs the collar of my shirt and pulls me toward her, then with her, as she backs away from the wall. She doesn't take her lips off mine until she stops and spins us around, then pushes me on the couch.

Her sudden aggressive stance has me worried that I might not even make it out of the gate, let alone to the show, seeing as once she left, so did my carnal desires. They were replaced only with an insatiable want for her return.

To prevent this from occurring, I start doing what I always do in times like this. In my head, I start mentally disassembling the only love that's never left me: My bike.

But this time is different, because as I'm disassembling, she's disrobing.

And with every article of clothing that drops away, the picture of me removing bolts and fasteners also disappears. And now, all I can think about are her gentle curves and supple breasts that are on full display in front of me as she climbs into my lap.

I feel myself straining against my jeans, the pressure mounting with each roll of her hips as she grinds herself against me. I put my hands around her waist and pull her firmly down onto me.

I stop kissing her, pull her close, and whisper into her ear, "You have no idea how many nights the possibility of this never happening again haunted me. I need to feel you, Kitty. Right now."

And with that, I take control. I roll her off of me onto the couch and stand up, quickly undoing my leather belt and unbuttoning my jeans. I was never a fan of tight-fitting clothes, and in this moment I remember why.

I kick my jeans and boxers off in one quick motion, not wasting any time. I need to be inside her. There's nothing more I can think about. At this point, I don't care if I last ten hours or ten seconds. I just need to feel her warmth enveloping me.

She follows my lead, and I watch her undress. She slides her shorts down, revealing a lacy black thong underneath her fishnet stockings just before she kicks the shorts across the room.

She knew this was gonna happen, and she dressed for the occasion.

And my god, Kitty, you are the only woman I know that can look so good in so little.

I can't stand it any longer. I take up the space between us with a quickness, kneeling down in front of her and running my hands up her legs. The fishnet grazes against my fingertips as I work my way up to her waistband. I take a hold of her stockings and panties in one grip, and decide there's no room for patience or a light touch. With one motion, I tear them from her body, hearing the lace and knit give way, like a sigh of defeat.

Now, the sudden brutish urge has overtaken me, and Kitty's prior control is no longer existent. I decide that the soft couch is no place for this, and I pull her to my face, inhaling the familiar scent that only comes when Kitty wants to come. Reluctantly, after a long exhale, my hands cup her lower back as I guide her down beside me.

Almost as if in a trance, she allows me to lower her to the floor, something she's never done before. Kitty always needed some sort of pedestal, even if was only a couch or a bed. And until now, I granted her that.

But not tonight.

As Kitty touches bottom, she moves to lie back. But I stop her, repositioning her on her hands and knees. She always insisted I was too big for her for this position, but what she never seemed to consider was the endless fantasy it would bring me, just by seeing her like this. With her normally reserved and bookish character now gone, she becomes my ultimate vision of a sexual goddess.

I make my way behind her, grabbing a handful of her hair as I pull her toward me. I feel her quiver as my tip presses against her. She's already wet. With a little more effort, I slide into that delicate area nestled between her thighs, inch by inch. She shudders before I'm fully inside of her, letting out a small squeal of surprise.

Normally I hold back until I feel her relax enough to accommodate my length, but right now, I have to feel myself deep inside of her. I still have a handful of her hair, and I firmly draw her back upon me. Her body puts up a bit of resistance at first, unintentionally making it difficult to accommodate me all the way to my base. And I wonder, briefly, if she has been waiting for only me to fill her.

After a few encouraging thrusts, her squeals become moans as she tightens around my shaft, and I know her well enough to know that she's on the brink of coming. But I'm torn, because while I don't want this to end so quickly, making Kitty come is damn near the closest to god that I've ever been.

I increase the pace of my thrusts based on the noises she's making, no longer worried if I'm being too rough due to how wet she is. I slide my hand out of her hair and onto the back of her neck, nudging her toward the carpet as her perky little ass juts up in the air. I look down and watch myself slide in and out of her, wondering how such a petite girl can handle me in such a feral state. At this point, she's pressed face down, and I can feel myself grinding her into the carpet. I know this because my own knees are feeling the rug burn. But having Kitty tightly wrapped around me dulls any sense of discomfort.

Her moans erupt into screams of pleasure, and she comes, hard, clenching around me.

But I'm not done yet.

As her body gives way, I roll her over onto her back. Another favorite position of mine, because with each thrust, I can watch her breasts rise and fall as she melts into a pool of pure satisfaction.

After what seems like hours, and another successful orgasm on Kitty's part, I feel myself approaching the edge of no return.

"I'm gonna come," I tell her.

She wraps her legs tighter around me, and with the sultriest voice I've ever heard, she says, "Come for me, Joey."

10

JULY 20, 1:37AM

Kitty

The shade of blue you refuse to wear,
it would look so good on you.
I wanted to cover you in remorse,
paint your lips with apologies that never came.
I wanted to forgive you.

I wanted ~~to cover~~ you ~~in remorse,~~
~~Paint your lips with~~ apologies ~~that~~ never came.
This shade of blue ~~you refuse to wear,~~
~~it~~ would look so good on you.
But I can't forgive you if you never ask me to.

HE PULLS me closer in the shower as we're rinsing off.

I playfully back away. "You ripped my panties," I tell him, stating the obvious.

He laughs, and the sound is a gift, his smile making me remember the intense gaze he had just an hour and change prior.

So different than this one now, so relaxed and easy. So…content.

"I'll buy you new ones. But there's a catch. You have to promise I get to take each of them off you, at least once," he says.

I'm damn near panting at the thought of it. And I do what I always do when it comes to him. I give in. "Fine," I tell him. "But only before the summer ends."

It's my attempt to stop this before it begins. Before it goes too far.

But has it already?

Is this the start of a fresh break? A scar I'm picking at?

Maybe…maybe this can just be about sex. Maybe we can just do what we've always been good at.

Maybe I can lie to myself a little longer, if only to enjoy him. Here, in the water, I can't count all the feelings. Maybe it's better that way.

He pulls me closer again and this time I let him.

"You have to save at least one pair for the fall," he whispers.

I know I can't promise that. So I say nothing. Because while I know I cannot allow myself to be consumed by him once again, I'm not strong enough to deny him in this moment. Not after what just happened between us.

I can wait to ruin this. He can wait to ruin me.

Again.

Because I know he will.

He has proven capable of doing so. It's one of his super powers, the masterful way he knows how to disarm and destroy me.

I'm grateful he can't read my thoughts, because his mind is still elsewhere as he speaks into my ear.

"I love it when I make you come. When you come soft. When you come so hard you can't speak. I love all of it," he says.

"And when I ask you to stop? So it's not too much?"

"It's never too much," he tells me, the shower water glistening off his face, dripping from his nose.

He pulls my hips in to meet his and shuts me up before I can say anything else, bringing his lips to my own.

But when we part, I can't help it. The mention of the word *love* has veered me off course, already. "I don't think love is supposed to be as intense as ours was," I tell him. "I've read about it, still do. All the time. No books ever mention…*this*."

"We were never written about, Kitty."

With that, he grabs my hands and holds them still as he pulls me into him, pressing himself against me. And even with the shower water raining upon us, I know a certain wetness is strictly because of him.

"How do you even know it was ever love between us?" I ask him bluntly, too physically fatigued to try to dance around the question that's been burning in my mind for the last two years.

"Love?" he says, like it's something he's never had to question. His hands slide over my hips, my thighs, as his head bends down to meet my other lips.

"Love," I repeat, like it's foreign to him. I grab at his hair with my hands he's now freed. Like he's given me permission to do so.

Like I'm the one in charge here.

His tongue meets my opening, the one I can't speak from. The one he speaks to most freely. Most regularly. Even when he isn't trying.

"If this isn't love, I don't know what the fuck is," he says, before he starts his romantic assault on me.

I tilt my head back, the shower steam hitting me with a force that tells me to shut the fuck up and enjoy this.

And then, all the poetry I've written for him, all the words I've strewn together, they all come out through his motions.

Through the way his tongue slowly circles my clit.

Through the way he grabs my ass and slightly lifts me in the air, encouraging me to come deeper into his mouth.

Through the way he moans as I come, like this is his art and I, the muse.

Part of me wants to stop him. I want to stop him and ask him if *this* is the kind of love either of us want. The kind we need. Yearn for. Live for.

I want to ask him if it's the kind of love either of us deserve.

But the climax I'm on the verge of, it doesn't let me.

It doesn't let me stop him.

Not when I want to.

Not when I need to.

Not even before I come so hard, that I think I might ruin his immaculate face.

I just let him worship me.

And in turn, I worship him. By the way I respond to him. By the way I need him so badly I think I might fucking die if he takes his beautiful mouth off of me.

And it dawns on me, then. How being here, now, with him, simultaneously feels like everything has changed, yet nothing has changed.

11

JULY 20, 2:13AM

Joey

I'M LYING in bed with a naked Kitty draped over me, her one leg slung over me in that way she's always preferred. Her breasts are against my ribs and part of my chest, her eyes fluttering closed as she drifts off to sleep.

I'm studying her face, her curves. The way her fingers occasionally twitch as she fights sleep.

But I'm not ready to close my eyes for the night. I'm not ready for this sight to dissipate behind the closed curtains of my eyelids.

It's a moment I have to remind myself is real. A moment I waited for, for so long. Too long. And as much as I don't want to seem needy, or desperate, I fucking am. For her. And I need her to know, before she even attempts to sneak out in the middle of the night after freaking out about what just went down between us.

Because that's what Kitty does.

She runs.

And when anything overwhelms her, or scares her, she bolts the first chance she gets.

"Kitty," I whisper, my hands playing with her long brown hair.

"Hm," she says, eyes still closed, her hand resting on my stomach.

"I need to know what this means to you," I say, hating it. The way I sound like every hopeful chick that's ever said that same exact thing to me after what I just considered a quick lay. My heart catches in my chest, hoping her next words are words in the same realm that I'm in.

"Joey, let's just go to sleep," she says, after a pause that I notice. "It's late."

I stop playing with her hair and grab her hand, giving it a gentle squeeze. "It's late but it's not too late."

She finally opens her eyes and looks at me. "What are you getting at here?"

"What do you mean?" I ask, sitting up.

"You want to know what I mean, or what *this* means?" she says, gesturing between us.

"Both."

She sighs, frustrated. "Look, we've always had great chemistry. It's undeniable. It's been undeniable from the start. I don't know, I saw you, and I just…"

"What?" I say, cutting her off. "You just wanted to do this one more time, for old times' sake? Or do you want to try again with us?"

"I could never say just one more time. One more time with

you would never be enough. I don't know what the future holds, honestly. All I know is, I'm here for the summer. I'd like to spend it with you. Just…in secret."

"In secret?" I ask her, letting out a small laugh. "What, so, you'll come over here to get laid real quick and then go back home? We don't go out? We don't…"

"Joey, stop," she says, pressing a finger to my lips. "My sisters would seriously go ape shit if they knew I was even here right now. I don't *want* it to be a secret. We can go out sometimes. You just, you can't come to the house. Or the bookstore. I'm serious. Promise me."

I groan out a sigh of my own. "Fine. But only because your sisters are crazy."

She laughs and slaps my arm. "They're not crazy. They care about me. Maybe just a little…too much."

"You're still not answering my question, though," I remind her.

"Which is?"

"Us. What do you want to happen with us? Is this your way of telling me you want to try again? Because I do. I want that."

She hesitates before she responds. "I don't know. Can we just, enjoy each other for now? And worry about the rest later?"

I'm half tempted to tell her no. That it's all or nothing. The same words she's used on me in the past. I want to tell her that I want all of her or none of her.

But I can't, because it isn't true.

If Kitty needs to pretend this is just fun, that we're not finally heading toward our future again, then I'll let her live in that bubble. For now.

"Sure," I say. "We'll worry about the rest later."

I watch her fall asleep, all the while, I'm worrying about it now.

And then, it feels like I've only just blinked my eyes as I wake up in the morning.

And Kitty is already gone.

12

JULY 20, 9:44AM

Kitty

Three orchids for three of the days you spent waiting to see me.
Three hours for you to make me forget my own resolve.
Flowers for a crimson dawn.
A eulogy for my conviction.
A testament to how far the slightest forgiveness can go.
And I forgot to ask you,
where does all the bad go then?
And where has all the good gone?

AS I WHEEL the cart of new releases that I need to stock to the front of our bookstore, I avoid the glaring and questioning gazes of my sisters and wait for the interrogation that's sure to come.

Lucy sits at the register, feet up on the front counter since no customers are in here this early. Sophie is standing beside her, doing some paperwork.

"You never came home last night," Lucy says.

Here it comes.

I keep my eyes on the books in front of me, busying my hands. "I told you not to wait up."

"Don't you think we should at least know where you're sleeping? And if you're safe?" Lucy replies.

I can feel her eyes burning holes into my back. Damn Lucy with her trick questions and making me feel guilty. But she's right. "I'm sorry I didn't let you know I was okay. But you guys need to remember that I'm nineteen now. You don't need to know my every whereabout."

Sophie clears her throat, a common thing she does to get my attention when she thinks I'm avoiding a subject.

"Look at me," Sophie says.

Shit. Shit. Shit.

I turn around defensively and put my hands on my hips, looking her straight in the eye.

"Were you with Joey?" Sophie asks, not taking the long way there.

I look back at the books I was stocking before I answer, knowing I can't look at her if I have to lie to her. "This conversation is over. I don't want to talk about him anymore. How many times do I have to tell you that?"

"We had to watch you become a broken goddamn mess after you ended it with him. It took too long to pick up the pieces. I already said it, but I'll say it again, and from experience, mind you. You should never return to an old high school love. You need to leave that shit in the past, where it belongs. Do you want to be in love with some dude headed for jail like I was? I swear to god, Kitty, I won't let you go down that road,"

Sophie warns.

I hardly have a rebuttal, after being lectured from her on the countless nights I spent crying and pining over him. "I'm not stupid," is all I can muster in response. But I don't even believe it myself.

I can't look at Sophie, knowing the hell she's been through with her own first love, and admit to making similar mistakes. Lucky for her, though, when we came back, Seth was long gone. He's still a ghost. She doesn't understand what it's like to come face to face with someone in the present that you gave your past to. She's the lucky one here; she moved on.

"I don't hear you denying it," Lucy says.

She has this way of speaking in a tone that only edges on anger, making me miscalculate where we stand in any conversation. But the way she's looking at me—and I'd know it even with my back turned—a pointed gaze that doesn't let up, tells me I'm not off the hook.

I turn around and stare at them both. "I'm not getting back together with him. I'm not going back down that road," I say. "I already promised myself I wouldn't, even if I wanted to. So don't worry."

"Okay," is all Lucy says, finally taking her eyes off of me, like she's satisfied with the finality of my response.

Sophie, the more easygoing of my two sisters, walks over to me and starts helping me put the new books up on the display I'm working on.

"Well, look at the bright side, Kitty. He inspired some poetry in you and got you writing more, right? Just, leave it at that and let it go. For your own good," she says.

I offer a weak smile in response, glad to close the conversation at that.

And I appreciate that she's lost the judging tone. But I hate the fact that they hate him. Solely because of me.

Sometimes, I wish I'd never confided in them about the darkest parts of our relationship. The lies. His reckless lifestyle and all the ways he wounded me.

If I could go back in time and change anything about all this, it wouldn't be my leaving. It would be the way I handled the disclosure of information about my relationship with my sisters.

Because once people who love you know about all the bad, they refuse to acknowledge any good there ever was.

And for all Joey's bad, he had a lot of good in him.

They also made it crystal clear that they would never stand for any sort of reconciliation between me and him.

It's exactly why I have to keep this to myself. Because I don't know why I decided to meet him at that show.

I don't know why I have such a weakness when it comes to him.

I don't know if I'm lying to myself when I tell myself our last encounter was purely sexual and devoid of any emotion. Could it ever be? Once emotion has entered the mix?

I change the subject once and for all and look at each of my sisters. "Well, what about you two? Why are we only talking about me? Any hot summer romances for either of you that I should know about?"

Neither of them look at me as they quickly say "No" in unison and get back to work.

13

JULY 22, 9:02PM

Kitty

I lost you like a limb.
A part of me, tethered,
something I thought I'd have forever.
I carved your initials inside of my heart,
left a permanent engraving.
Our goodbye was left in my marrow,
in every aching part of me still longing for you.
I wonder if I would have missed you like this
had I never known you.
I wonder if you could miss a person you never truly knew.
The way comfort sounds, it's just noise.
It's mere background music to my thoughts of you.

I PULL up outside Joey's house and see his bike and truck both in the driveway. The lights are on and I try to breathe out both the relief and the butterflies.

I shaved before coming here.

This is what my sisters warned me of.

I told myself I wouldn't get swallowed by him again. I told myself I could stay away if I viewed this as something less than what it was in the past.

But I wasn't thinking about that when I took a shower earlier. I wasn't being smart when I decided to show up at his place, unannounced and uninvited.

But I know, regardless of the time that's passed, that I'm always welcome here.

That I'm always *wanted* here.

He's said it enough times. And by the tone of the conversation he started when I was last here, he still feels that way.

I don't use the rational part of my brain when it comes to him. All common sense ceases to exist and then I am telling my sisters I'm going to the movies.

And then I'm pulling out of my driveway and into his.

I get out of my car and walk up the path to his front door, where I knock to the tune of *Push It* by Salt N' Pepa—our signature code.

I couldn't stand the fighting anymore, between Sophie and Lucy. Their harsh words aimed at each other. The details they keep excluding me from. It all sounds like misplaced anger and bitching to me, and it's too loud. And since they don't seem to want to let me in on what they're really fighting about, I saw myself out.

I just wanted peace.

That's a lie.

Part of me wanted peace, and part of me wanted…

"Hi," I say as he opens the door—shirtless. I swallow the grin that's taking over my face as I take the sight of him in.

His low-rise jeans. His boxers peeking out of the top of them. The defined V of his abdomen. His arms. How I've missed those arms.

How feeling them wrapped around me reignited a hunger I foolishly thought had lessened because of time and distance.

He swings open the door for me to come in and after I fully appreciate the sight of him, I notice his face is not the happy face I thought I'd see.

But I walk inside anyway.

"Hi," he says, sitting on the couch and lighting a cigarette. "Wasn't sure if you'd be back or not."

Oh, right.

"I called an Uber in the morning and left before you got up. I didn't want my sisters worrying about where I was," I tell him.

He nods, exhaling smoke, and I can tell he's hurt.

I touch his arm. "Joey..."

But he shrugs it away from me. "Kitty, I don't know if I can do this the way you want to do this. If you stay over here, I want to wake up with you here."

I nod. "Okay. I'll stay." I run through a stream of expletives in my head as I curse myself for giving in, yet again. If he would have put a damn shirt on, maybe I could have refused.

But if that simple request is what he needs to be okay with my conditions, I will grant it to him.

I almost forgot how needy he was. For me, for security, for *us*.

Only Joey could be such a rebel and a romantic. Only he could crack my ribs with his smile.

He looks at me and his face softens. "Okay," he says, a smirk finally creasing his face before he puts his cigarette down in the ashtray on the coffee table. "Now get the fuck over here."

He grabs me and pulls me onto his lap, giving me the hello I thought I'd initially get. Our lips and tongues meet in a vicious need and before I know it, he's pulled my shirt off and I'm fumbling with the button on his jeans.

This certain kind of passion is so delicious, but so dangerous. It ropes you in just before it hangs you.

And you never see it coming.

Maybe that's the fun in it. The thing we all chase.

In my case, time and time again.

I've died a thousand deaths with Joey and here I am, wrists out, begging for him to bind them once more.

14

JULY 22, 11:58PM

Joey

"TELL ME EVERYTHING," I say to her, as she's rolled over on her side staring up at me with those beautiful brown eyes.

Laughing, she says, "What do you mean?"

"I mean what were you doing in all that time you were gone? What's new? What's different? What's changed?" I ask.

My appetite to learn everything about this version of her is bottomless. The Kitty that's here now is different than the one who left. This Kitty is older, more guarded if it's even possible, and protective. What she's protecting, I've yet to find out.

"I don't know," she says, looking down, playing with a loose thread on my comforter. "That's a lot of time to try to summarize really quick."

"Will you try for me?" I ask her. "It doesn't have to be quick."

"Well, let's see. I left. Lived in a new place for the first time in my entire life. It made me realize how big the world is, how small I allowed myself to remain by staying here, not growing, not evolving. I started writing more. More poetry. Some short stories here and there, but I don't know, there's something about poetry that just moves me. It just falls out of me sometimes. More so after I left you."

I nod, encouraging her to go on.

"And I've been trying to figure out what I want to do with my life, but it doesn't feel that simple. You know, I'm nineteen now. I feel like I should have it all figured out at this point. But I just don't. All I know is I want the words to always come. I want the poetry to always be there, whether it's spilling out of me or my life. I want the words to be beautiful. I want my *life* to be beautiful. In every aspect of every single thing, I want nothing less than magnificence." She turns to me. "Sounds dumb, doesn't it?"

"Not at all." And it doesn't. The optimist in her, the dreamer, it draws me in. Such a contrast to the pessimistic and nihilistic way I often view things, at least when she isn't around. "It sounds like leaving me inspired you in certain ways," I say. What I don't say is how much that hurts me, how it kills me to think she might be better off without me.

"It inspired the melancholy," she says, almost like she regrets that fact. "And for some reason, sadness is such a better muse than happiness."

"Seems like it. You didn't write that much when we were together," I say.

"Not true," she says. "I just never shared it with you."

I sit up a bit to face her. "Why not? I would have liked to read it."

"No, you wouldn't have."

"Why do you think that?" I ask, probing for the truth she doesn't want to admit.

"Because it wasn't all happy stuff. In the beginning, sure. You inspired some of my most cheesy poems. Blocks of swiss, if you will. But after time, it changed. The poems got darker, more intense, more honest. It would have hurt you to know how much you were hurting me," she states.

"Maybe it would have sped up the change I made for you," I counter.

"Or maybe it would have pushed you to another extreme, knowing how deeply your lifestyle was impacting me. Maybe you would have been the one to leave," she says.

I shake my head and look at her. "I would never leave you."

A look of guilt passes over her face. "It doesn't matter. I may have left you, but you were still with me. All this time, you were still with me," she says quietly.

"There was no one else?" I ask, the question I've been dreading asking.

She laughs. "No. Who could follow in your footsteps, Joey Madden?"

I don't even try to suppress the grin that's taking over my face at this new information. "I don't know, but no one could follow in yours, either. It was a lonely two years, I'll tell you that. The porn was getting old."

Her face changes and she grabs mine. "Wait, you mean, you haven't been with anyone else? This whole time?"

"Nope. Embarrassing, I know," I admit.

"Why?" she asks, with a look of shock. "What if I never came back?"

"I don't know," I say, shrugging. "I guess I was just holding on to the idea that you would be back. That I'd have a chance to fix things with us. Your sister was still here. I knew at the very least you'd come to visit."

I don't tell her that I've had eyes and ears on the street since the moment she disappeared. I don't tell her that I've had watchdogs on corners. Friends of friends of the Bordeaus. I don't tell her I was going to make damn sure I'd see her when she returned, whether she was interested or not.

And I don't remind her that I deserved at least a goodbye. But it's on the tip of my tongue, wanting to come out.

"And is that what this is to you?" she asks. "Your way of trying to fix things with us?"

"No. I did the fixing while you were gone. My way of doing that was changing my entire life for you. I got out of the club. I stopped all the shady shit. I wanted to be the man you wanted me to be by the time you came home," I tell her. "So I became him."

A tear forms in her eye and she wipes it away before it can fall. "You really stopped everything?"

"Yeah. Because I love you way more than all the shit you ever hated," I say, hoping she knows I mean it. "I'm sorry it took me so long. And I'm sorry you ever had a sad thing to write about."

"I'm not," she says. "Not sorry about the writing, I mean. It helped me. With you I learned what I did and didn't want in a relationship. It's funny how you gave me both. I'll always appreciate it. Even the bad."

I take her words in for a moment before I speak next. "You know, you leaving, without saying goodbye, that shit really hurt, Kitty. Why didn't you at least tell me you were done? Why didn't you give me any sort of warning or heads up?"

"I'd been telling you for so long that I was done, or would be done if things didn't change, that those words had no meaning anymore. And I knew I couldn't look at you and say goodbye. The cycle would just repeat, as it always did. Plus, you were metaphorically severing that tie with us for so long, it finally gave way."

"That wasn't the right way to handle it," I say quietly.

"Maybe not," she says. "I've thought about it, a lot. I'm sorry it hurt you. But I need you to know it hurt me, too. And I'm sorry I felt like I had no choice but to leave like that."

"I may not like it, but I can understand why you did it. Just please, don't ever do that to me again," I tell her.

Looking into my eyes, she says, "Don't give me a reason to, and I won't. I promise."

"I won't," I tell her. Finally feeling a certain release of bitterness, I try to lighten the mood and take a risk. "What do you say we start fresh? Get to know the new and improved versions of each other?"

She grins and climbs onto my lap. "I don't know…is this seat taken?"

15

JULY 27, 6:34PM

Kitty

For a moment we slipped and said what we meant.
The truth has a way of escaping the things we say
when the earth falls away.
When masks slip and feelings drip.
When your hand in mine
means more to me
than all the ways you hurt me in the past.
And I see it now. The thing that scares me most.
Rock, paper, scissors, shoot.
I choose you.
Every time, I'll choose you.
And I'm afraid that someday,
you won't choose me.

WE PULL into the restaurant parking lot and I wait for Joey to park the bike before I swing my leg over the side and hop down. I'm silently praying no one will be here that knows either of my sisters, but when he asked me out for dinner with a hopeful look on his face, I couldn't say no.

He's been trying—*really* trying—to show me how important I am to him. To make things right between us. He keeps using the word "again" but to me, it's the first time things have ever been even close to a positive place with us.

After the initial glamour faded from the honeymoon phase, I saw what kind of life he really lived. The decisions he made. The danger he put himself in, daily, and in turn, me, by association and attachment.

But tonight, two years after I severed our romance with a butcher knife and no goodbye, he reaches for my hand, and I let him take it.

He leads me inside the crowded Italian restaurant and the hostess seats us in a corner booth.

He's wearing a button-down shirt and a familiar, comfortable smile.

I would have opted for my sleeveless black dress, but he insisted we take the bike, so I'm in booties, skinny jeans, and a three-quarter sleeve top.

He reaches across the table, searching for my hand once more.

"Thank you for letting me take you out," he says.

"Don't flatter yourself, I only came for the Alfredo," I tease.

He laughs. "I'm serious. It means a lot to me. That we're here together right now."

I squeeze his hand. "Me too."

After what feels like a heap of food in my stomach and

relaxed conversation, I think the night is about to wind down, but Joey says he has a surprise for me.

I give him a curious stare and raise an eyebrow before I try to get it out of him what it is. But his response lacks any real answer, and he tells me to just get on the bike and hold on.

We pull up to another restaurant/bar type of place, off the lake. I haven't been here before. It seems new, like they opened it at some point while I was gone.

He grabs my hand for the third time tonight and with an eager face says, "You ready?"

"For what, exactly?" I ask nervously.

As we reach the entrance, I see there's a chalkboard sign outside that reads **Poetry Slam/Open Mic. All voices welcome.**

I instantly freeze where I'm standing and grip his arm with my other hand. "Joey," I say cautiously, staring at the sign and blinking, "what are you doing?"

"It's time you share your words with the world, darlin'," he says, like it's nothing, like it's no big deal.

Meanwhile, the anxiety buzzing in my chest is almost enough to make me go into cardiac arrest right on the spot. I've never read my words aloud. I've never shared my words with anyone. Not even my sisters.

I never said I was ready for this.

I never said I *wanted* this.

"I can't do that," I tell him, drawing the line.

Dinner? Fine. Being seen in public together? Okay. This? Absolutely not.

"Oh, you can," he says. "And you will."

"Or what?" I ask, challenging him. My face is as serious as my question and my hesitation.

"Or I'll throw you over my shoulder and carry you to that stage myself," he says, just as seriously.

And the unfortunate part is I know he isn't joking. He really would do that shit.

"Why are you doing this to me?" I ask him. "I don't want to do this."

"Because I believe in you. And I want to hear every sad word even if it hurts me, if it means you'll finally open yourself up to the world."

I shake my head, frightened tears threatening to spill.

"Come on, Kitty. You can't hide forever," he says. "Now, are we walking in calmly, or am I carrying you?"

When I don't respond, he moves to pick me up.

"Okay! Okay. We're walking," I say, reluctantly.

As we reach the outside patio, there's a string of white lights stretching from the back of the building to the front. There's a long dock nearby leading out to the water, with an even longer section of the beach in close range. I see people walking along the water's edge, sitting on the sand. Couples star gazing and enjoying the summer moon.

Someone is on the mic, reading a piece they've written. Performing, really. It's theatrical, impressive, and very…beyond whatever skill level I may have achieved, if you can even call it that.

There's a signup sheet in the far corner that Joey damn near pulls me to. I stand in front of it, staring, and he interrupts my daze by handing me the pen.

My hand is shaking as I write my name on the list, and then it's fumbling through my crossover body bag to find my phone as I follow Joey to the small crowd.

There are tables on the patio, filled with patrons and other poets, I imagine. Knowing I'm in the presence of other writers, about to read my work aloud, gives me a certain sense of discomfort and fear that I've never known.

Please tell me I have a decent poem saved in my notes in here to read.

I am frantic and scrolling, reading over my words that now seem so juvenile, so cliché.

I don't know if I've been searching for five, ten, fifteen, twenty minutes, when my name is called on the mic.

I hardly have time to make a quick decision as I pull up the one haphazardly labeled "Beach" in my phone. And I just pray it's decent, or relevant, or god, just not that fucking horrible and embarrassing.

Joey is clapping loudly, and whistling, as I make my way to the mic.

I step toward it, trying not to trip over myself, probably looking like a nervous idiot already. "Hi," I mumble into the mic, lowering it so it reaches me. "Um, I'm Kitty Bordeau. The piece I'm about to read for you is called *The Beach*. I hope you enjoy it."

I bring my phone to chest-level and then, I don't think. I don't have time to. I just read.

"I wrote about you through the pain, through the loss, through everything you left behind in me.

I breathed you in through every memory, felt you in every heart palpitation left in your absence.

I never wanted your phantom hands to stop touching me, in every way, on every day.

At some point, they did.

The memories became dreams I almost couldn't remember.

Some things were always better left unsaid.

'I miss you' was one of them. Wasn't it?

But it still lingers on my tongue, with every other unspoken word in my mouth meant for you.

I swallow them on the good days, choke on them on the bad.

Your razor smile doesn't go down so easily anymore.

It's a struggle, a scene, a laceration that doesn't quite stick.

Yet somehow, one I can't seem to heal from.

The wounds become wonders and you, the assailant, the surgeon, the savior.

Somewhere, you are still on a beach, waiting for me.

And I am waving hello or goodbye, I can't quite tell which anymore."

As I finish and look up, I see a woman's figure on the beach nearby, a short distance from the bar. *Is that Sophie?* I squint to see her better, but with the dim lights, I can't tell. I can just barely make out a male figure hovering close enough to her that they might be together.

But it can't be Sophie. If she was seeing someone, I'd know. She would have told me.

I realize I'm stalling my exit, so I put my phone down and look back up at the crowd, muttering a "Thank you" into the mic before rushing off the stage, where Joey scoops me up in his arms.

16

JULY 27, 9:49PM

"YOU DID AMAZING, KITTY," I tell her, holding tightly onto her once I finish swinging her around. "I'm so proud of you."

I set her down and hold her a few paces back from me, so I can really look at her. I'm studying her face, her posture, her aura…

And she interrupts me and says, "What the hell are you doing?"

"I'm just trying to see if you look different with all that brave all over you," I say.

She smacks my arm and it doesn't hurt at all. "Shut up!" she whines. "I hate you for making me do that, you know."

"Do you now?" I ask.

She's always been a shit liar.

"I do," she insists, but the gleam in her eye says otherwise.

"Uh huh. Well, the crowd didn't hate it."

She smirks and tilts her head in mock adoration. "Oh, stop. You flatter me."

I slide all jokes aside and look at her. "I'm serious. It was really good. I think you should do this kind of thing again."

"You're biased because you like me," she says, avoiding the serious bit in conversation like she usually does when it pertains to her.

I grab her by the belt loop in her jeans and pull her closer to me. "First of all, I don't like you, I *love* you. Second of all, the spotlight looks good on you. I think that's where you should be, and I think I can share you with the rest of the world. You and those beautiful words."

She smells like flowers and shampoo and I feel like holding her this close to me forever. As I finally exhale, she wraps her arms around my neck.

"Sorry to break the spell, kid, but I've read an awful lot, and my words aren't that beautiful," she says solemnly. "They were just typed on a whim after a dream. They weren't even meant to see the light of day."

I shake my head and let out a disgruntled sigh. "It kills me that you don't know how special you are," I tell her.

She smiles at me but it's full of sadness, her eyes full of self-doubt and self-consciousness. "No one's special, Joey. They just think they are. That's the trick."

"What is?" I ask, confused.

"Once you start thinking you're special, that you're really *someone*, you lose any magic you may have had. You become just another person thinking they've earned something. That you're entitled to whatever good happens to you." She pauses. "I never want to be one of those people. So please, for my own sake, don't ever try to convince me I'm special again."

Judging by her somber tone, I decide not to argue with her on this one. Only she has no idea that viewing the world in this way makes her that much more impressive in my eyes.

"Fine, Kitty. You're not special. You're regular. So fucking regular," I say.

Then I grab her and pull her toward me and kiss her, so she can feel how much she means to me. And right now, I don't give a damn who's here. I don't care who sees, if they tell her sisters, if they think we're together or back together or if she's smack dab in the middle of a new mistake with me.

I just kiss her.

For as long as she lets me.

17

JULY 28, 10:18AM

Kitty

Depression is a great white shark.
It feeds. It feeds.
Depression is a vicious host.
It needs. It needs.
Depression is a stark white room.
I clean. I clean.

I'M TIDYING up the bookstore when I stumble upon a book by one of my favorite authors, Kat Savage. I pick it up, opening to a randomly selected page.

I read a few passages and my heart fills when I stop on one in particular.

"I start to think about all the people who have disappeared from my life. Sometimes with a goodbye, sometimes under a cloak of darkness, *and sometimes without even looking in the rearview at what they left behind. I've been destroyed by too many goodbyes with no one nearby to build me back up. People don't stay. We are nomadic at our cores."*

I dog-ear it for the next reader, then close it and put it back on the shelf.

These words, I think. *These words are beautiful.*

Mine could never compare.

Comparison is a plague, I know. My sisters have told me so. But I can't help it. The authors I admire, the ones I respect, I don't know where their talent stems from. How it flows from them so naturally. They make pain and beauty feel effortless.

I can't help but envy it.

Even when I convince myself it's a waste of time. Even when I know, deep down, that I'll never be like any of them.

After the open mic, I felt different things.

Elated.

Proud.

Stupid.

Embarrassed.

Invincible, despite it all.

When I left Joey's this morning and returned to the watchful and caring eyes of my sisters, I felt something else entirely.

Guilt.

Treachery.

Foolishness.

Lucy was making a cup of tea as I walked through the front door as quietly as I could. She said nothing to me as I made my way upstairs to the bathroom closest to my bedroom. I didn't give her much choice, hightailing it out of her line of sight before she could ask me where I'd been.

I'd sent the courtesy text the night before, letting her and

Sophie know I was okay. But somehow it didn't feel like enough. In my heart, I know it's not right. Keeping this from them. Hiding away the truth where they can't see it. Knowing that I've done the exact thing they warned me against. That I've let my heart lead me to where my head can't save me.

I just wanted to wash the feelings of inadequacy away. That annoying burn of remorse and wishing you were never born.

I don't know why it comes. I never have.

One moment, I can be fine.

The next, I am miles away from fine, searching for a street sign to point me in the right direction.

I never find it.

This is when I often find myself writing. The worthlessness, it grabs ahold of me, rings me by the neck until that's all I believe in.

I try to scribble it out. I jot words down, trying to appease the little monster. It becomes a show and tell of my worst fears and thoughts, audience of one.

The applause never comes.

The curtain never drops.

No flowers at my feet.

And I am left standing there, alone on the stage, wondering where to go next.

Depression is a greedy thing, a blood-thirsty guest.

And how can you tell someone you love that something is wrong when you can't pinpoint it yourself?

Instead, you search for the venom. In your veins. In your very core. In the parts of you that you cannot even reach.

And the monster turns around—*you can feel him smiling at you, where is he?*—and he laughs at you for trying to find him.

He laughs and he laughs, and as you hear the echoes getting farther away, you start over again.

On a brand new day.

In the same place. In the same crawling skin. With the same face.

I've always convinced myself it had something to do with my youth. I let my sisters in my head enough times that I think everything will get better with age. That every bad thing will fade in time.

That my immaturity will run out at some point. That just maybe, it might really grow legs and run away from me.

I don't believe in the tooth fairy but I believe in my sisters, faeries in their own right. Those two little magical beings with wisdom sprouting from their heads. I believe in their words. The things they tell me in effort to make me believe that life will get better, easier, as time goes on.

Sophie is twenty-eight years old now, with some therapy under her belt for her own personal strife and grief. She constantly reminds me that we can overcome these things if we put the effort in. But real effort, not just wishing for it to change and not doing anything about it.

Lucy, twenty-six, says that life has a way of humbling you before kissing you on the mouth. And that every answer she ever needed could be found in a book.

I imagine our mom would have told us that life can be anything we make it.

Our dad probably would have told us to go out there, grab the mold, and break it.

I hardly remember them anymore.

All I have are memories my sisters reminisce over without me, seeing as I was too young to recall them, and photographs I stare at by myself, creating memories of my own.

The illusions are almost as pretty as I imagine our lives were once, before it was all ripped away.

Before the monster came to play.

"Kitty!" Sophie calls out, interrupting my unwelcome spiral. "Get your little ass in here, please? I need your help with this sign."

"Coming," I reply. I grab the duster and head toward her voice, recognizing it as the safety it is.

18

AUGUST 1, 7:29PM

Joey

IT'S BEEN days since I've heard from Kitty and I wonder if she's rethinking this, or if she's in one of her phases. Where she doesn't want to talk anyone, see anyone, even me. She has a tendency to slip inside herself occasionally, retreat from those she cares about. She hasn't shown up here, and she made it clear that I can't show up at her house.

Correction, I wasn't *supposed* to show up at her house.

When we were together, I'd try to pull her out of herself. Sometimes, it worked. Other times, I simply had to wait it out.

Earlier today, when I knew her sisters would likely not be home, I slipped a letter in their mailbox for her. I tried to disguise my handwriting, knowing Lucy would probably tear that shit up before it ever reached Kitty's hands.

But I had no other choice. Kitty's been refusing to give me

her new number, and still has me blocked on the few social media apps we both have, insisting that we need to take this "slowly" or we run the risk of becoming attached to each other's hips again.

I disagreed, but went along with it to appease her. Personally, there's nothing more I'd like than to be attached to her hip. Or another body part of hers that I adore. But if time is what she needs, it's a small price to pay for the massive fuckups I've stacked in the past.

The note was short and to the point.

IOU. Panty shopping tonight. 7:30PM?

She probably figured I'd forget, but the sound of those stockings and her thong tearing is something I doubt will ever leave my mind for good.

I'm sitting here, remembering the way her ass bounced in the air as I entered her from behind, when there's a knock on my door.

I smile at the old ridiculous tune she still knocks to and yell out for her. "It's open."

In she walks, like she owns the place, and she might as well. She still owns me, that's for damn sure.

"Panty shopping?" she asks with a smile, walking over to where I sit on the couch.

I grab her and hoist her onto my lap, kissing her slowly, madly, before I stop to finally respond. "Yeah. Panty shopping on a Thursday. It's totally normal. Don't make it weird."

She laughs. "Are they for me or for you?"

"Me, duh. I want something that says…I want you, but not too desperately. Something racy, but sophisticated. After all, I'm not that kind of girl." I turn my head like I'm whipping hair I don't have.

"You're an idiot," she says, then she grabs my face and brings it back to her and kisses me again.

"You gonna try 'em on for me?" I ask her when our lips part, reaching my hands around to cup her ass.

"No," she says, breathing a bit heavier before removing herself from my lap and now growing erection at the thought of her in nothing but underwear. "We better get going before we get distracted." She eyes my hard dick.

"Oh, this old thing?" I point at my jeans.

She laughs and grabs my hand, pulling me up. "Come on, Joey. Stop trying to seduce me."

"Why, Kitty?" I whisper into her ear, before kissing her neck and gently nibbling on her earlobe.

She exhales and puts her hands on my arms. "Because it's gonna work. Now let's go." She releases her hold on me and walks toward the door, turning around as her hand touches the knob. "Do you have your keys? Let's take the bike. It's beautiful out."

I grab my backpack, keys, and her helmet and we head outside. I start up the bike and wait for Kitty to situate herself behind me. When she wraps her arms around my waist and squeezes, signaling that she's ready, I grin.

There's nothing better than having a beautiful woman on your bike, holding onto you like this. And that woman being the love of your life, well, it's something every man dreams of. I look up at the clear summer sky, wondering how the fuck I got so lucky, before I swing us around and pull out of the driveway.

When we reach the store, I park the bike and wait for her to hop off. She hangs her helmet on the left foot-peg and I grab her hand as we head inside.

"How fancy you tryin' to get?" I ask her, eyeing up the lingerie once we make entry.

A blush unfolds on her cheeks and she says, "I'll make you a deal. You can pick out one thing you want to see me in, but I choose the undies."

Christmas fucking morning, I think, heading for the good stuff. I turn around, still walking backwards and yell out to her, "You're a size perfect, right?"

She laughs, clearly embarrassed when other patrons turn to look at us, and shakes her head. "Small, you doofus."

About fifteen minutes later, I've found it. A black, one-piece, complicated, whatever you call it. It's very revealing, very hot, and very much something I want to see Kitty in. I'm all but drooling at the thought of taking it off of her.

I'm also wondering how the hell she's going to get it on with all these damn strings everywhere like it's some kind of Pinterest project.

I find her in the panties section and hold up the nightiemajig to her, pretty proud of myself.

She smiles and looks at it, turning it around to thoroughly check it out. "Whatever floats your boat. A deal's a deal."

She holds up a five-pack of lacy thongs with about a one-inch strip of fabric going all around the top of them, with all different colors. "These'll do for me," she says.

"I approve," I say, squeezing her ass with my free hand.

She slips her hand in my back pocket and I pay for her things before we head home.

Who would have known underwear shopping was such good foreplay?

By the time we get home and she slips into the little black number I picked out for her, I admire her in it before taking it off her—with her guidance, of course.

I'm a mechanic not a magician.

But I devote my hands and energy to pleasing her as many times as I can before she tells me she has to go.

Once she's dressed and I have my pants on, I grab the bag with her panties still in it, taking them out.

"Wearer's choice," I say, holding them up. "Pick a color."

"Hmm," she says, eyeing the colors. "The baby blue. Why?"

"We had a deal, remember. I get to take each of these off you, at least once. But the baby blue pair you have to save for the fall. No wearing them until then."

She smirks and grabs the panties from me, then puts them in her bag. "We'll just have to see about that."

Then, she kisses me before she heads home.

Once the door closes, I'm already wondering when I'll see her again and which color panties she'll wear first.

19
AUGUST 1, 11:11PM

Kitty

*Meet me where the storm meets the horizon,
where pride releases its grip on our throats,
where doubts deflate and hearts are finally sure of what they want.
Take me to a place where standing your ground
means more in the end
than being buried beneath it,
where you don't swallow your dreams
and choke on another's expectations,
where you don't punish yourself for failing yourself,
where you hope for naught
and want for all.
Find me in the rose garden there,
sprinkling silent thanks
for every hell I had to live through*

in order to make it there.

"YO, KITTY KAT," Sophie calls from the living room as I walk in and close the front door behind me.

I put my keys down on the kitchen counter and join my sisters on the couch, plopping down between them. I lay my head on Sophie's lap and stretch my legs over Lucy's. Sophie starts playing with my hair as I do so.

"Do you guys think people can change?" I ask, looking up at the ceiling. "I mean, really change. Entire lifestyles. All bad habits included."

Sophie remains still, but her face tells me she's thinking about how to respond.

Or maybe she just wants to roll her eyes. I'm never quite sure with her.

"I'd say it depends on the person," Lucy answers.

"Dependent on what, exactly?" I ask her.

Lucy takes a moment to think before she answers. "On whether they acknowledge who they were and embrace who they've become," she finally says.

I take in her words while thinking about Joey, wishing I could just come straight out and talk to them about him. I briefly consider telling them the truth. I don't recall a single time in my life I've ever made a decision without at least one of my sisters' input or advice.

It's hard knowing what to do when I'm lacking their guidance.

Maybe they've been right this whole time. Maybe I am still incapable of making my own choices. Maybe it's not that they still feel the need to lead me, but that I need them to.

"Why do you ask?" Lucy asks.

I shrug. "Just something I was thinking about, I guess."

Lucy looks at me, like she's deciphering whether or not I'm telling the truth. She's always been the pensive one, processing her words internally and logically before putting them together in a form that soothes, stings, or pulls.

"Bullshit," Sophie says. "Spit it out."

Sophie, on the other hand, has always had a way of sucking the information right out of my soul. I think it has something to do with the intensity of her stare, like she's daring me to lie to her or pretend nothing is wrong.

Both of them have this certain *something* that draws the truth from me. Maybe it's the fact that the same blood runs in our veins. Maybe it's the bond we've built throughout our lives, through beauty and loss and tragedy and growing into women. Maybe it's just a thing with sisters. That they seem to just *know*. Even when you don't want them to.

I settle on telling them part of the truth. A part they can live with. And me, considering I'd be headless if they knew I was sneaking around behind their backs to go see Joey.

"I don't know. I heard through the grapevine that Joey's changed. That he's different now. Got out of the motorcycle club and has his head on straight," I say.

For a brief moment, Lucy and Sophie look at each other—but it's not so brief that I don't catch it.

"Wait," I say. "What was that? You guys just looked at each other like there's something you know that I don't."

Sophie fumbles over her words momentarily before regaining her footing. "There wasn't a look. Do you hear yourself right now? We've been home for a little over a month, and you're already thinking of going back to him. Why? Why not date someone new? Can you just not help yourself with him at all? I get it, I've been there. But at some point, you just have to let high school shit go."

I look down in shame and shrug, unable to admit that no, I can't help myself. I have no defenses against Joey Madden, no immune system. And worse, I have no desire to stray from him.

Being back in this town only makes it worse. The distance he covers, the places we've been—together—he's everywhere. And he's constantly calling to me.

"I just think about him sometimes, and if things could be different now that's he's out of that shit lifestyle," I say softly.

Lucy leans forward, her lips parted as if she's tasted her words and decided they're perfectly ripe for the occasion. "I do think people can change. And I think beautiful people in the world—like you—can wish change for everyone. But I'm not convinced that Joseph Madden is capable of turning his life around. My concern is for you, having loved and left him…and *me*. I don't want to see that happen again. Not when I've witnessed him hanging around with that rough crowd, making a mess of the town while you've been gone." She places firm fingers on my knee. "Some people are worth the risk. And others…they'll just keep burning you until there's nothing left to light."

Her words snag on my heart and I breathe out in response. I try to think of a way to defend him, but I know better, and it lodges in my throat. No matter what I might try to say, they would use sound reasoning to prove me wrong. And I wouldn't be able to argue. Because you can't argue with the truth, even when you don't want to believe it.

But the good in him, I think. *All that good. It's still in there. If only you guys would try to see it.*

"She's right, Kitty," Sophie says. "Now, stop thinking about him. Go write a hate poem about him or something and remember why you left him to begin with. Lucille and I have a few things we have to talk about."

"When are you guys gonna tell me what's going on with the bookstore? I know something's up. I heard that guy who came in the other day and offered to buy it," I say.

A glance is shot between them again.

"There's nothing to worry about, Kitty," Lucy says.

I exhale again, this time louder and more purposeful, and I stand from the couch. "All right then, keep your secrets," I say, mimicking the popular meme floating around the internet we always send to one another.

"Goodnight, ass hat," Sophie says, laughing.

"We love you," Lucy calls to my back, since I'm already walking away.

"Love you guys, too!" I yell.

I make my way upstairs to my bedroom and sit on my bed. Taking out the new pack of panties Joey bought for me, I stare at the baby blue pair, turning them over and over in my hands. I graze my fingertips against the lace, thinking about how easy it is to tear things to shreds. Love is such a delicate thing in careless human hands. So easy to fumble with and destroy.

I wonder if my sisters might be wrong this time. I wonder if Joey and I really can make it to fall.

The more I'm around this version of him, the more I think I'd like us to.

20

AUGUST 3, 7:32PM

Joey

MY CELL PHONE vibrates in my pocket, so I throw the dirty rag over my shoulder and slide out from under the Chevy Blazer I'm working on.

I look at the familiar name lighting up my screen and wonder what he wants. We don't talk much since I left the club, but to me, an old friend is still a friend regardless.

"Mickey," I say, answering the phone with a grin as I stand and light a cigarette, leaning against the hood. "Long time no bullshit. What's up?"

"Joey fuckin' Madden," he says with a slight laugh in his voice. "It has been a long time. The guys miss you, man."

I tilt my head back and repress the words I've already repeated to him countless times. I substitute them for the truth instead. "I'd be lying if I said I didn't miss you guys too sometimes. But, it's gotta be this way. I told you that."

"I know, I know. So, you straighten your life out yet like you wanted to?" he asks me.

"I'm getting there," I tell him. "Keeping my hands clean has certainly helped."

"Yeah, about that..."

I look around to make sure no one's in ear range before I inquire what he's getting at, knowing that's about to change. "What's up?"

"Well, you know how no one gave you too much shit about getting out besides blacking that ink on your leg? It's time to return one of those favors you promised us," Mickey says.

Fuck. I swallow hard, hoping it's nothing too crazy. The last favor involved a very sketchy and very risky drug run. I swore it was my last good deed for the club. But with this life, you never know what your last errand will be, or if it will be your last act in general on this god forsaken planet.

"What do you need?" I ask him, biting the bullet.

"A couple of hot heads from a new local MC threatened to shoot up our clubhouse to Dylan's old lady. We're gonna go over to their little shack and pay 'em a visit."

"Come on, man. This rival shit always ends badly. You know it," I try.

"We need the muscle, Joey. And you always knew how to throw a punch," he states.

"Yeah, where'd the muscle get Skully?" I ask him, reminding him of our friend who's been six feet under since this revenge shit granted him two bullets in the head.

He was rewarded with his nickname after death.

It was around the time I realized this life was not just for fun, or brotherhood.

Silence on the other line. And then, "That was different."

"How, Mickey?" I ask. "How was that any fucking different than this? It's an endless cycle. We go there, they'll come to Cherry Cove, and then what? Who dies next? One of the guys, one of their wives? A fucking kid? A neighbor?"

"You owe us. Be at the clubhouse at nine tonight. We ride out at midnight. End of discussion."

I hear the silence again, fully aware that he's hung up and the conversation is over. I don't have a choice in the matter. I signed my life away to the club, even upon getting out of it. Some blood never washes away. Sometimes, even when you try, your hands will never be wiped clean of your past.

I go inside to shower. Afterwards, I grab my blade from my drawer and slip it into my pocket before heading out. I may know how to throw a punch, but I also know that some of these guys might be fighting with way more than just their hands. Cherry Cove MC members included.

———

AFTER ALL THIS TIME, they've still got my cut behind the counter for times like this. Mickey comes over to greet me, shoving it against my chest when I reach the bar after walking inside.

"Glad you showed up," he says roughly.

I nod, even though we both know it wasn't really optional. Still, he gives me a hard hug.

"Get this stranger a beer, will ya?" he shouts over his shoulder.

I grab the bottle after Missy slides it over to me. One of the local crew girls.

"You're lookin' real good, Joey," she says, eyeing me suggestively, no morsel of shame or shyness in her voice. "What are you doing later?"

"Not you, sweetheart," I tell her, an apology in my tone. "I'm flattered, but I'm spoken for these days."

"Ugh, still?" she whines, bringing a laugh out of me.

"For as long as she'll have me."

She pours us two shots. "Well, I'll be damned. A faithful fucking man. I'll drink to that."

I drink mine back after we clink our shot glasses together and turn around to my name being called.

I always have a bit of hesitation when I'm back in the clubhouse as a non-member. I may have left on the best terms as I could have, given the entire situation, but you never know what mood the guys will be in, who might be too drunk or outspoken, who might think I'm a pussy or worse, a traitor. And one thing I do know is none of them take a shine to outsiders, especially the newer members I don't know.

But, I don't know if it's better or worse that most of them aren't getting wrecked before we head out.

It tells me that they're serious about this. Serious enough to stay mostly sober.

And when the VP pulls us in to discuss the little surprise get-together get-down, I know we're heading into a whole lot of shit I've been trying to stay away from.

We head out into the lot at the same time. Thirteen members total, plus me. We start our bikes and ride out at midnight, as planned. Two of the guys bring the van, and knowing what's inside, I nearly change my mind. A little voice inside tells me to turn around, but I ignore it.

Because I have to.

21
AUGUST 4, 8:08AM

Kitty

The hidden monster in you is selfish and reckless, wrecking us for fun.
The hidden monster in me is starved and voracious for you,
snaking us into one.
She's a rabid dog that likes you most,
licking your scraps and wounds while snarling at me.
She is traitorous and tempted,
still howling for you, still crawling to you.
I can't leash this sick love,
it is constantly breaking and bending for you.
You are unmoving, the firm hand for the wild heart that thrashes.
The hidden monster in you,
the lifeblood to our living and breathing tragedy that thrives,
he is so buried, so safe, so warm,
you don't even recognize him as grotesque anymore.

I'm a slave to mine.
His and hers,
you're the master of both.
You are still taming her as she's still maiming me.
And I am still learning that I cannot outrun either of you.

I COME DOWNSTAIRS to find Lucy at the kitchen table. She's reading the morning paper with her signature cup of tea on the table, the tea bag resting on the surface, likely driving Sophie nuts as usual.

I walk over to each of them and give them a kiss on their head. Lucy puts the newspaper down as I do so.

"Morning," I say with a smile, grabbing my favorite mug from the cupboard before heading toward the coffee pot.

"Kitty, you should sit down," Lucy says, placing her hands on the paper.

I wrinkle my brow at her as I pour my coffee. "Why, exactly?" I ask, still with a half-smile, only out of curiosity this time. But something in her tone tells me this won't be a pleasant conversation.

My sisters only tell me to sit down when they think I can't handle something. When they think news might upset or enrage me—and I've been known to suddenly react both ways. I can't help it. My temper knows no bounds. It comes quick, but it can depart just as fast.

When Lucy doesn't respond, I look at Soph for some sort of hint. Her eyes meet mine before falling on nothing in front of her, telling me she doesn't want to be the one to say it.

"Just, sit," Lucy says. "Please."

Her eyes are begging and sorry and the fear takes hold of me.

I add in my creamer and sit across from Sophie, then lean toward Lucy who's sitting at the head of the table.

"What is it? You're scaring me," I say.

I want to fidget with my fingers or hair but I remind myself I am not five anymore and my nervous tics don't get me anywhere.

Lucy looks at Sophie who nods silently. "It's Joseph," Lucy starts.

My heart starts pounding in my chest. *Please, don't let him be dead. Please tell me he's okay.* "Wh-what about him?" I stutter. "Is he okay?" I want to rush to her, snatch the paper from beneath her guarding hands. Another part of me is dreading what she's about to say next. I want to run, flee from whatever bad news is about to bombard me.

"He's okay. He's just been arrested," Lucy says.

I start shaking my head. "But I was just..."

With him, I almost say.

Lucy reads my eyes. "You were just...?"

"I was just thinking about him. Lately." My confusion bubbles over into anger and I know I need to put a lid on it before I react too emotionally in front of them. My rage will give me away. It always has. My sisters know when something pokes the soft part inside me that most people can't reach.

"I know," Sophie says. "I know you're upset. I'm sorry he's found a way to disappoint you yet again, even from a distance. I knew he would."

"Let me see the paper," I say flatly.

Lucy slides it over to me and I turn it over. The headline reads *Local MC Rivalry Goes Awry*.

I shudder and brace myself before I read the article, which states that fourteen members of the Cherry Cove motorcycle club were arrested shortly after midnight last night. The time of arrests was twelve thirty-seven AM, and there were so few police officers and so many members, they had to use zip ties to arrest them in a line until more cops arrived.

Apparently, they set out to not only beat the shit out of some rival crew members, but they also decided to set their little clubhouse on fire.

Charges include arson, assault with deadly weapons, battery, breaking and entering, and possession of deadly weapons.

I put the paper down and rest my chin in my hands, covering my own mouth to prevent hateful words from spilling out.

He said he was out.

He said he was done with this shit.

Sometimes people pretend they are who you want them to be.

Sometimes you believe it.

I close my eyes and try to stop the tears from coming.

"Are you okay?" Lucy asks, reaching across the table to touch my arm.

"Just disappointed," I manage. "At least no one was killed this time." I force a fake smile and swallow the hurt.

"That's not fucking funny," Sophie snaps.

"It wasn't meant to be," I say. "And this is the part where you guys say you told me so, right? That I was just being naïve, as usual?"

"No," Lucy insists. "This is where we commend your big heart. There's nothing wrong with wanting to see the good in people, despite all the bad."

"You have a big heart, Kitty. I just want to stop seeing it break. I can't take it anymore," Sophie says.

I nod. "I'm gonna go upstairs. I'm sorry. I just..."

"We know," Lucy says. "Take your time. If you don't feel like going into work today, take the day off."

"Thanks," I say, standing from the table, grabbing the paper. "Do you mind if I take this?"

"Go ahead," Lucy says.

"Read it as many times as you need to for it to sink in that he'll never change. He's just like Seth. And look where Seth is," Sophie says.

"Thanks for that," I say, hating that she is once again comparing Joey to her first love who's currently in jail for breaking and entering. But, as usual, I think there's more to the story than what she's told me.

"I just don't want you to keep getting hurt," Sophie says.

"I think that's inevitable in life," I remind her, turning and heading upstairs with the paper in one hand and my coffee in the other.

When I reach my room, I close the door behind me, even though what I really want to do is slam it and throw my mug at the wall until it shatters. So it matches my insides. So it's louder than the breaking inside me.

I sit on my bed and read the article approximately ten more times.

I stare, and I simmer, and I set. And I surmise that Joey said all the right things to squirm his way back inside. And it worked. Stupid me, it fucking worked.

Maybe I am young. Naïve. Foolish.

Maybe my heart chases things it could never truly capture.

Maybe I never had a chance at getting any of this life shit right.

But what I do know, in this moment, is that Joey is still a liar. He will still tell me the things I want to hear, the things I so desperately want to believe. He will grab my fears, turn them around on me, use them against me. He will continue taking my softness and forgiveness from me for as long as I let him.

And I can no longer allow it.

When people continuously let you down, you have to change tactics in order to survive. Sometimes, that means pushing them from the cliff of your disappointment.

When possible, you need to kill the monster. Every one you can reach.

I fold the paper and finish my coffee, staring out the window by my bed.

It dawns on me that it's time for me to grow up and focus on the one person I've been neglecting my whole life. The person I continuously put everyone else before.

Myself.

22
AUGUST 5, 12:16PM

Joey

GETTING BAILED out is easy when you commit crimes with a large group of people. I'm still kicking myself for going, still hating myself even more for bringing the blade. Now I got a nice new charge under my belt and I'm sure Kitty has heard about it by now. And not just her, but her sisters. If they have any say in it, Kitty will never speak to me again.

I can't say I blame them, or her. I know what this looks like. I know I fucked up. And I know if you ever admit your wrongdoings and then follow it with a "but" it pretty much negates whatever came before it. But…I didn't have much of a choice in this. I just hope Kitty gives me a chance to explain that.

I would rather spend a year in jail than consider the possibility of spending the rest of my life without her.

I don't have to see her or talk to her to know what she's

thinking. I'm sure she is beyond pissed. I know—knowing her—she has already made up her mind about me. That she thinks every single true thing I told her was just more bullshit. More lies.

I have to convince her this entire mess isn't what it seems.

But it's hard to argue with facts, and I know Kitty will throw every single one in my face. I just hope I can get to her before her sisters do, if they haven't already.

I know if I ever really want this to work between me and Kitty, I have to get her sisters to come around. But that's a task for a later date.

Right now, I just need Kitty to understand what happened.

I start my bike, this time with no weapons on me, just a sorry fucking note and a plea for the opportunity to explain what happened.

Once I arrive at Kitty's, I open the mailbox and place the envelope inside. No cars are in the driveway, and I know where at least one of them are right now, if not all of them.

I'm not sure I'm mentally prepared to face the wrath of the Bordeau sisters, but fuck it. I made this bed. Eventually, I'm going to have to lie in it.

With this in mind, I head to *Bordeau Books*.

I pull up on the street and realize I'm starting to sweat.

I peer through the storefront.

Right behind the front counter sits Lucy. The one who hates me most.

Fuck. Does the woman ever take lunch?!

Who I don't see right away, is Sophie, until she's charging at the door with a pissed off look on her face.

God, they're all so scary.

I almost wish I wore my helmet so she wouldn't recognize me.

"What in the actual fuck are you doing here?" Sophie says as she storms over to me.

Judging by the look on her face, she already knows about the arrest.

"Sophie, it's not what you think," I say, calmly. "I'm just here to see Kitty. Please."

"Well, not only do we not want her to see you, but *she* doesn't want to see you," Sophie says. "You should go now."

"I am very aware of how you and Lucy feel, trust me. But maybe you should let Kitty decide if she wants to see me or not," I say, biting back the words I really want to say. This is not the first time her sisters have tried to dictate our outcome, but I'll be fucking damned if I let them do it again.

"Joseph, listen. I'm aware we coddled her for longer than we should have. But all we did this time is show her the evidence. It was in the goddamn paper. What'd you think, that she was going to come back here and ruin her reputation by hooking up with you again? No. She's smarter than that."

I just nod, and while I want to tell her she's wrong, I'm not sure that she is. And at this point, I know better than to argue with any of the Bordeau girls. "Fine, Sophie. You're right. You have me all figured out. You and Lucy always have, haven't you? You decided who I was before you ever even really got to know me. That was real nice to do to Kitty, by the way. It sure has made her confident in her choices when it comes to us, knowing how much her sisters have always supported us and all." I turn to walk away, but I turn back. "And you know what else? She *is* smart. Smart enough to make her own decisions. Have a good day."

And with that, I get on my bike to take off before she can say any more words that might succeed in convincing me Kitty is better off without me.

But I stop at the sound of her voice.

"Hey, Joey," Sophie yells. "Prove us wrong then."

I can't help the slight smile that comes. Because Sophie doesn't know that's all I need.

The chance to do so.

The hope that her sisters just might let me this time.

23
AUGUST 10, 9:14PM

Kitty

Without you, I am restless and morose.
With you, I am alone and adrift.
A fisherman's goodbye, left behind.
A warning of departure
and a promise to return that never came.
Certain words didn't fall from your mouth.
Your absence reminds me of those that fell from mine,
predicting this careless farewell.
You made a fortune teller out of me.
I made a false god out of you.

A BROKEN HEART can really push you to some strange places. I've been processing, accepting, and attempting to heal for almost a week. Notes, flowers, apology cards, they've been coming nonstop from Joey. Yet again, he's trying to tamper with my feelings. My resistance to his bullshit. While it's difficult to ignore him, it's not impossible. I am reminded—daily now—of why I left him to begin with.

The murder of his friend back then, the violence now, it still exists. He is not outside of it the way he led me to believe. And for the second time, I need to save myself.

And I hate him for making me choose.

Now, I'm sitting in a place I haven't sat in since I was a kid.

The teepee in our living room, the one my sisters never took down. Maybe it reminds them of when we were little. Maybe it helps them remember the good.

I used to live in this thing when I was younger. It was my safe place.

I always had a thing for forts. The hiding, being shielded, something about it comforted me.

Maybe the reality is I've always been trying to hide from myself.

Maybe eventually, if you're lucky and you look hard enough, you can find yourself.

As I jot the thought down in my notebook, I hear rustling on the outside of the teepee. I look up to find Sophie crawling inside with me.

I quickly shut the notebook and move aside to make room for her.

"Whatcha doin' in here, Kitty Kat?" she asks me.

"Just writing," I say.

"You haven't been in here in years."

"I know," I reply. "I guess I just wanted to feel like myself again. Sounds silly, doesn't it?"

"Nope," Sophie says. She points to the notebook. "What kind of shit is spillin' out of that head?"

I shrug. "I feel like you and Lucy have everything all figured out, and I'm just...here. Always the one trying to understand this adult thing, what I want for my life, my future, if I even have one."

"Kitty, come on, you have a future. Close your eyes and envision your perfect life. What's it look like?" she asks.

"Sophie..."

"I'm fuckin' serious, just do it."

I let out a sigh and close my eyes.

"Good. Now, think about your version of your perfect life. What do you see?"

Joey. Two kids. Our children running around with my sisters and their kids. A career as an author.

"I see myself marrying the love of my life," I say sadly. "Our two children. You, Lucy, the kids you both have. I see myself as an author, someone who was really able to make writing their life." I stop and play with my fingers. "I see someone who didn't just dream it all up. Someone who made that dream a reality."

"Well, go make it then," Sophie says.

"What?' I ask her, looking up after I open my eyes.

"Create *that* future. The one you just thought of," she replies. "Only you can do it."

I look at her and can't help it. I lunge. I fling myself into her arms and hug her, so hard, so tight, I think I might break us both. "Thank you," I say, because it's overdue.

Because for every moment I have been alive, she has been living partially for me.

I get up as much as I can and climb out of the little teepee, heading straight for the garage. I search through boxes, tearing them open, looking for my old journals. Looking for the things I've written over the years. The things that have shaped me.

The things that could help shape my future. Because within Sophie's advice, was clarity.

I need to stop hiding.

I need to put a poetry book together, and put it out in the world.

I reach a plastic container and open it up. But when I grab a stack of letters, with my name on it, in every possible variation, I freeze.

This is Joey's handwriting.

I tear open the first letter in the stack. The date on it is not even a week after I left to go live with Sophie, two years ago.

In it, he is begging for a reason. As to why I left. If I will answer him. If I am even reading this. If I hate him so much I wouldn't ever give him a proper goodbye.

If I ever loved him at all.

In the third letter, he is begging for my forgiveness.

In the seventh letter, he sounds defeated.

In the thirteenth letter, he is apologizing for still writing, for still caring so much.

In the twentieth letter, he says he loves me more than he loves himself. And he's getting out of the club.

I stop at the next letter, where he says he will never stop trying. Where he says he will never stop loving me, even for leaving him so he could better himself.

By the time I fold them up again, I am burning up. With anger. Hurt. Disappointment.

How could my sisters keep this from me?

How could they let me cry, all those days, thinking Joey didn't even care that I left?

How could they watch me suffer like that?

I grab the handful of envelopes that are spilling over my

hands and storm back into the living room. Sophie is in there. Lucy is in the adjoining kitchen.

I toss the stack on the kitchen table. "Is there anything either of you would like to tell me?" I ask, venomously.

"Where'd you find those?" Sophie whispers, joining us in the kitchen.

"It doesn't matter where I found them. It matters why you hid them, why you kept them from me. Both of you," I say, glaring at both of my sisters.

"You were still a kid," Sophie says. "You have to understand, it was our job, to…"

"To what?" I yell. "To break my heart even more than it was already breaking? To keep my fucking boyfriend from contacting me?"

"You were seventeen," Lucy says. "You wouldn't have understood. It would've confused you."

"If that's your excuse, my *age*, I turned eighteen after I left. I became a fucking adult. You tried to decide my future for me!" I yell, tears blurring my vision. "It wasn't your choice! It was mine! You took that from me! You took my entire life from me, every chance you could!"

"We took your life? No. We were trying to protect you," Sophie says.

"When will either of you realize you can't protect me from everything? Worse, you can't even protect me from yourselves," I say, spitting the words out. Then, I take a deep breath and rub the hurt from my throat, looking straight at Sophie. "You know, it's funny. Here you are, trying to help me mold my *bright future*, when in reality, you stole two years from my past. You tried to mold my future for me. You didn't even stop to think to ask me what I wanted. Like it was your life, not mine."

Sophie doesn't have a chance to respond before Lucy grabs her arm and interjects.

"Kitty," Lucy starts, "we were trying to do what we thought was best for you."

"Because you always know what's best for me. Even better than I do, right?" I say to her. Then I look at Sophie again, tears blurring my eyes. "How could you watch me cry, every day? How could you keep this from me? Lucy, she was here. You, you were *right there*."

"Kitty, I..."

I hold my hand up to stop Sophie from continuing. "No. I'm done listening to either of you right now. The funny thing is, I thought I could trust you both with everything. I can only imagine what else you've been hiding from me."

With that, I grab the stack of letters and head upstairs to my bedroom, where I slam the door, trying to slam them both out of my life.

All I want right now—as the rage and sorrow tear me apart, fighting to prove which is stronger—is Joey. Joey and his arms around me.

Joey and his search for forgiveness.

Joey and my granting of it.

Joey and my remorse for not giving it to him sooner. Joey and his remorse for not asking for it before it was too late.

My stupid heart betrays me every time; me, and all the logic my brain conjures up to keep us at war.

24

AUGUST 17, 10:13PM

Kitty

> *My body is waterlogged and weary,*
> *heavy and caged.*
> *Every conversation with you held me captive.*
> *Each moment led to certain surrender.*
> *I was your submissive, your prisoner.*
> *You, my demise disguised as my saving grace.*

SPENDING the remainder of the summer without Joey makes me feel like there's a drought in my life.

I've almost sought refuge from the thirst by running back into his arms.

But I know, despite how brutally I miss him, I need to stay away from him.

And as much as I wish I had my sisters to turn to, I just don't. Part of it is due to their overall absence. Part of it has to do with our blow-up, which led to some serious questioning and hurt feelings on my end.

I've been keeping to myself lately. I ripped my head from the clouds, violently, and started viewing life and every aspect as what it is, not what I want it to be.

It's difficult, altering your way of thinking. I've tried to bury my desire for getting what I want. I've tried to accept that sometimes, things just aren't how you want them to be.

I'm also learning that if you want things to change, you have to sometimes shake them until they do. Until some sort of fruit falls from the tree. Even if it's rotten.

Even in my anger and hurt and disappointment, I've been clinging to Sophie's advice. This notion that I can create my future, piece it together until everything I see fits.

After I came down from the peak of Mount Pissy, I went searching for my old journals again. And I found them. They were buried at the bottom of a box marked *Kitty's Random Stuff*. I shook my head at how unoriginal it was, the irony of the box holding a writer's life's work, wondering if the handwriting was my own.

I wasn't surprised that I covered the journals with other, less meaningful things. Children's books, yearbooks, silly drawings I made as a kid that my sisters wouldn't let me throw out. They liked the nostalgia of it all, I think, and holding onto that part of my childhood for as long as they could.

It was another reminder that I have always been hiding this part of myself, always afraid that I would never measure up to what I thought was good enough. Skilled enough. Poetic enough.

I burned the fear away, tried to banish the voice that

convinces me I'm not good enough. It's still there, but I ignore it now. The less power I give it, the less it has over me.

I dug through journal after journal, searching for old poems that I could be proud of today when I couldn't find it in myself to feel it back then.

To my surprise, between a handful of pieces from my early teen years and what I wrote over the last two years, there were enough for a decently sized poetry collection.

Over eighty pieces, varying in length and emotion, that I've since been compiling into a word document on my laptop.

Perks of being part of the book world have shown me that I'm not as lost as I always thought I was. Thanks to a bunch of indie authors I follow, and authors we have relationships with because of our bookstore, I know there's an entire world of self-publishing out there that will grant me the space and freedom to publish my words exactly as I want them.

One day, I might try to go the traditional route. But right now, I know in my heart that this is the road I want to travel on.

And regardless of the outcome, I will have done it on my own. I don't care how many copies this book sells. I don't care if it doesn't sell a single one, to be honest.

All I care about is proving to myself that I could do this, and so I did.

My train of thought is interrupted by a soft knock on my bedroom door and I wonder which of my sisters it is, or if it's both.

"Come in," I call.

And I don't close my laptop. If they want to see how my pain transformed over the years, the shape it took in the form of poetry, I'll let them.

I swing around in my chair and see Lucy's slender frame in the doorway.

"Do you have a moment?" she asks.

"For you? Always," I say. Because despite my disappointment, my immense love for her could never disappear.

She comes in and sits on the edge of my bed, and her hands aren't empty. "I wanted to apologize for keeping the letters from you. It was never my intention to make you feel helpless or that I wasn't confident in your decision-making skills."

"I appreciate that," I say, meaning it. "I know you guys always want the best for me. I know it even when I'm angry at you."

"And I appreciate that," she says. "But there's more." She holds up her hands with the items in it.

Another bouquet of flowers.

Another letter.

"He keeps sending them," I tell her. "I've stopped checking the mailbox."

"I noticed." She places the items on the bed. "I'm sure you're aware that I was never a huge fan of Joseph Madden."

"You don't say," I tease, with a grin. "And I'm sure you know I never blamed you for that."

She smiles, and just like that, things are easy between us again. Then, her face gets solemn again. "I think I learned love from novels. And a love that ended earlier than anyone anticipated. Before I had a chance to pay attention to the balance of flaws and imperfections." She sighs and presses her palms into her thighs. "You two are human and mistakes will be made. My main concern is your happiness."

My heart swells in my chest at what sounds like a personal blessing from my older sister. For my choices, even if they may be potential mistakes in the making. "Lucy," I whine, walking over to her. I sit on her lap and throw my arms around her, hugging her with a gentle squeeze. "That means so much to me. Thank you."

"Yes, well, I've been learning a lot of lessons about judgment and forgiveness these days."

I wrinkle my face, wondering what she means.

Is this the same closed off Lucy that hardly lets anyone in her world?

Is there something I'm missing?

She taps my leg before I can say anything else. "Okay, up you go. I have a few things to take care of myself."

I rise from her lap and she takes my hands and kisses them both.

"Goodnight. I'm always proud of you," she says.

"I'm always more proud of you," I say, smiling, just before she winks at me and closes the door.

And I'm left standing there, alone, staring at the flowers and letter. I pick up the flowers and inhale the fresh, floral scent of the mixed bouquet. Then, I pick up the letter, turning it over and over in my hand.

But I still don't have the strength to read this one, or any other yet.

I know it will hurt too much.

25

AUGUST 26, 7:18PM

Joey

I FINISH what must be my hundredth fucking letter to Kitty in the last few weeks and put my pen down. I know I need to read over this one, at least twice. Kitty holds on to words, finds hidden meaning in almost every damn thing, even when there isn't any. I used to think it was a quirk. Now, I just want it to go away so it can make this even the slightest bit easier.

I feel like I'm losing my mind. I don't think anyone responds well internally to being ignored. And maybe externally, depending on the level of crazy in the individual.

I light up a cigarette and smooth out the paper in front of me.

My phone vibrates in my pocket and my heart starts beating a little faster. Each time it vibrates, or dings, I snatch it at the speed of light hoping that by some off chance, it might be Kitty.

But it never is.

Tonight's no different as I see Mickey's name lighting up the screen. I send him to voicemail—again.

I already told him, I'm done with the fucking favors. Done with the payback bullshit, in every sense. He told me they all think I've gotten soft, that I've given my whole life up for one pussy. It didn't sit well with me. Old habits die hard but hot tempers die even slower.

I may have threatened him with a crowbar and told him that he and every other excuse for a "man" who refers to women as merely pussy need to grow the fuck up and find a woman worth changing for. Then I called them a pitiful bunch of fucks who get hard off mental circle jerks they naïvely mistake for brotherhood.

Maybe I can get away from the violence, but it'll always be in me somewhere. Maybe anyone saying anything remotely bad about Kitty just brings it out of me.

I shove my phone back into my pocket and ash my cigarette, then stare at the letter and my chicken scratch handwriting.

Kitty,

For a petite little thing, you sure are vicious. I mean that in the nicest way possible. ~~Fuck,~~ *I'm already starting this one off wrong. I just meant that it's one of the things I've always loved about you. Your intensity, your ferocity. Your loyalty, to yourself above anyone else other than your family. Come to think of it, every single thing I love about you, that you are so firm and unwavering in, is also part of why you probably won't even read this.*

I don't know if you've ever read any of the sorry letters I sent you, or if you'll read this one now.

I can't say I like it, but I can say I respect it.

I will never pretend I didn't ever give you at least one real reason, if not an infinite amount, to cut me loose. But I also can't say I've ever stopped trying to give you at least one real reason to accept me back into your life. In any way you would have me.

I've begged for friendship, for even a fighting chance to be your acquaintance at some point. I've begged you to at least let me be someone you might see on the street and say hello to one day. I've begged for anything other than hatred. Because you are the single person in this world that I can't even stand the idea of hating me.

And that's the truth. In fact, it's the only truth I know at this point. Sounds pitiful, doesn't it?

But I guess that's what it feels like, meeting the love of your life and then feeling that crippling absence every day that they're gone.

To every letter, every miserable attempt at reaching you, I've received silence. A smarter man would have taken a hint by now and let you go. But a wiser man would have learned how to keep you in the first place. And not only keep you, but keep you happy.

And, to be honest, Kitty, I would settle for whatever you want just to have the chance to see you smile again. Even if it would kill me inside. But I can shoulder that burden. It's only fair. My shoulders are broader than yours, remember?

What I can't seem to accept, though, is letting you walk out of my life forever.

I know I've apologized a million times by now, for a million different things. For every way I've failed you. For every single time I ever disappointed you. For every time you cried because of me. For my carelessness, with you. For being the guy you didn't need but somehow the one you wanted. For fucking that all up, royally.

I won't lie. I don't ever want to stop trying to win you back. But, you're the writer here, not me. I don't have a way with words the way you do. And there are only so many different ways I can say I'm sorry before I have to accept that you just don't want to hear it.

So this will be my last letter to you. I can only respect your decision to distance yourself from me again. I just hope you never let me, or any other guy, change that beautiful heart of yours. I hope you never let anyone make you feel like you're anything less than fucking perfect. And I hope you continue making it hard for everyone in this shit world to get your attention, because for what it's worth, they should all be fighting for it.

I'm sorry I didn't appreciate it more when I had it. But I'll always want it back.

PS. You better go back to that place to read your poetry again. And even if you don't, just know that my spotlight will always be on you, Kitty.

I love you.

-Joey

I put my cigarette out and exhale, knowing for certain that this letter is likely pointless. If she hasn't responded to the others, what would make this one any different? But, I never said I was smart. I'm just an idiot who's not only lost the girl once, but twice, and maybe for good this time.

I fold the letter and put it in the envelope, licking it shut, knowing that even if she doesn't respond, if she at least reads it—even just this one—then she'll know how I feel about her.

I put it in my pocket and head outside to get the bike situated. I'm sure by now everyone on her street is sick and tired of hearing my motorcycle coming and going. But fuck them. It's not about them.

After I cruise the near fifteen minutes to reach her place on the lake, I take a deep breath and slip the letter in the mailbox, closing it before riding away from the Bordeau household.

As I turn around to watch Kitty's house fade in the distance, I wonder if I'll ever travel down this road again.

26
SEPTEMBER 2, 7:47AM

Kitty

A band-aid on the dam.
Gauze for this aching wound.
A smile plastered on my face
that holds nothing more than
pretending to be happy without you.
Is it convincing yet?
Everywhere it follows you,
the absence shadows me, too.
I run from it on the sand,
search for it in the water,
hold it close at night when I'm missing
your warm breath against my neck.
I've let myself get lost in this drunken cloud sway,
in this boring life without you,

but I still keep you with me
every day.

TODAY'S the big event at the bookstore, the one we've dubbed "Labor of Love: End of Summer Signing". We have a few big-name authors showing up to sign their books for readers, and poets coming to read; and I can't wait.

Watching the faces of readers as they meet their favorite authors, the looks on their faces, the tears in their eyes, the way they gush and laugh and hug and love, it's beautiful. It's inspiring. The way words can bring people together. The way they can captivate and hold you, move you. The way they can make you love an author you don't even know. The way they can make you feel like you *do* know them, like you are made from the same stuff.

Books are so personal.

Words are so unique to each person's experience, their view on life.

I can only hope to have any one of those effects on readers one day. I can only dream of having any readers at all.

But still, I can dream.

I'm getting the stacks of books in order at each table for the appropriate author. Lining up an assortment of sharpies, pens, and glitter pens for their choosing. Some of the authors have shown up, checked in, and left to get coffee before the chaos begins. But the whirring of excitement is already in the air. The energy that *Bordeau Books* is about to hold. It's magical.

Just as I start setting up and straightening chairs in front of the tables for the audience, for the poetry reading portion that will come first, I hear the familiar sound of a motorcycle pulling up out front.

Sophie and Lucy are busy tending to other things, but they

both hear it too, and they look at me with confusion and questions on their faces.

"What is he doing here?" Sophie asks. "I told him not to come back here."

"Wait, what?" I ask her. "When was he here?"

"Forget about that. Why is he here now? This event is too important to have him screw it up," Sophie says.

"I don't know why he's here," I say.

And just as I think I'm going to have a heart attack, I hear him say my name.

"Kitty."

I turn around and he's just stepped inside, looking slightly breathless.

I walk over to him, trying to appear calm, when inside my emotions are so conflicted that I feel like passing out or disappearing would be easiest. "Let's go talk outside," I say, grabbing his arm.

"No," he says, stopping me. "What I have to say to you, I want your sisters to hear too. And I have something to say to them."

"Okay," is all I can manage to say.

I step back from the closeness of him, his body heat. The scent of his body wash is too dangerous. And having him here, feeling him here, it's obvious in the way my body is reacting to him that I still have a weakness for him. Too many weaknesses.

Seeing him now makes me afraid that I might always willingly choose the weakness if it means I can keep him.

He rubs a hand on his head like he's searching for what to say.

"Wait, were you guys seeing each other this whole summer since we've been back?" Sophie asks. "Were you keeping this from us?"

"Oh, don't act like she's the only sister here with a secret," Joey says to her, pointing at her. "I saw you with that guy, on the beach. Who's he? Kitty never mentioned you were seeing someone."

I look at Sophie to see her reaction, but she just scratches her neck as her eyes widen like she's been busted.

"What guy?" Lucy asks her. Then she shakes her head and looks back at Joey. "That's not important right now. You have five minutes, Joseph," Lucy says. "We have too many things to prepare."

"All right, all right," he says. Then, he looks at me. "Kitty, I don't know if you've been getting my letters. I don't know if you've been reading them, or just ignoring them altogether. I don't blame you either way. I just wanted to tell you face-to-face, that what happened was not a choice I felt I had."

He goes on to explain the circumstances. How he owed the club residual favors for his permitted and peaceful exit from it. He tells me—and my sisters—exactly what happened. How it transpired.

How when the cop pushed his face into the ground with his boot he thought of me and how this would hurt me, and us. He speaks of the instant regret in his gut. The desire to take it back and make different choices. How he wishes he never agreed to owe them a single thing.

And how he told them that was the last time he would do anything even remotely illegal for them.

"Even when I try to do right by you, I fuck up," he says to me, getting on his knees and taking my hand. He looks up at me as he squeezes my hand. "But everything I do, every good thing at least, I do it for you. Because of you. I will sit here begging you like this, on my knees, until you believe me." Then he stands and turns to my sisters. "I know you guys probably don't, but it's the truth. I'm done with all that shit. Baby Bordeau here changed my life and me as a person, for the better. I'm sorry for not becoming the man she needed me to be sooner. But I'm here now. And if you give me the chance, I'll prove it to you. For the rest of my life if she'll let me."

He looks back at me, waiting for a response.

Tears form in my eyes before I can try to wish them away. And my mind goes blank with anything other than *yes*.

But I look at my sisters, waiting for their responses as he waits for mine. I wonder if they believe him. If they will support this rekindling of our crazy love for each other.

Sophie throws her hands up. "Fuck, he got me with that. That was some romantic shit. All right, Joey. If Kitty wants this, you better be good to her, or I'll fucking kill you."

Lucy laughs. "You know, that could rival some of the stuff in these romance novels, Joseph. Have you ever considered penning a book?"

He laughs and shakes his head, mouthing the words "Thank you" to them before turning back to me.

"So, what do you say? Is this seat taken or what?" he asks me, pointing to one of the empty chairs.

I grin and lunge myself into his arms. "It is," I whisper. "That damn seat will always belong to you."

EPILOGUE

OCTOBER 4, 10:23PM

Kitty

If you've never been to pier forty-two,
I can show you the way.
Grab your sweetheart, your muse.
And on their lips and sacred skin,
write all the words they inspire in you.
Even the ones you cannot find.
Especially the ones you cannot find.
Remind them of every single thing
that sent you tumbling into love with them.
And then, remember them all.
Even during the pitfalls.
Especially during the pitfalls.
Because although it's hard to find,
it's easy, too,

*to lose your way
back to pier forty-two.*

"JOEY!" I call from the bedroom.

"Yeah?" he yells back from the kitchen, where he's making me the sandwich I just asked for.

With extra fresh meat.

But I don't think he received my pun.

"If you don't hurry up I'm starting the next episode of Californication without you!" I yell.

"Wait for me! I'm coming!"

Little does he know I'd always wait for him. I wouldn't press *play* on a single thing without his presence beside me.

We've been binging the show from the start, for three weeks now. We're on season four, episode three.

In our relationship, we're on season ten, episode who-knows-I've-lost-track-of-the-days-because-I-am-in-bliss.

I sprawl myself out on the bed as seductively as I can manage, although being intentionally sexy isn't one of my strong suits. I try to spread eagle it and think again. Then I throw my legs in the air and start doing bicycle exercises for no real reason.

When I hear his approaching footsteps, I settle for lying on my side—elbow propped up on the bed, hand under my chin—and I toss my hair over my shoulder so it looks like it naturally got that way.

When he walks in, plate in hand, he smiles. "What are you up to?"

"Notice anything, stud?" I ask in the most porn-star-ish

voice I can muster, as I graze my fingers against the baby blue lace.

He sets the plate down on the nightstand and climbs into bed with me, crawling on top of me. He looks at my thong like he's thinking it over, touching it where my clit rests like he's trying to conjure up the answer.

"Our deal," he says finally, slipping his fingers inside the fabric where I'm already wet for him. "You really saved them for the fall." He smiles against my lips as he kisses me. Then, he stops all movement with his fingers and he looks at me. "Wait, is there a catch here?"

"Sort of," I say, removing my one hand from around his neck and reaching under my pillow. I pull out a new pack of panties. "How about a new deal? I'll let you take each of these off me if we can save the white pair for winter."

"Every season is for you, Kitty. With or without the thongs," he says, removing my underwear as he moves down my body, kissing me.

I lean my head back against the pillow and close my eyes, wondering how he makes the future feel like something I want to hopelessly fall into with him.

Kitty took one step forward in creating her future and published her poetry collection on October 16th. It includes the poetry found in this book, along with new pieces. To read it, please click the link below.

Read for free in Kindle Unlimited

ACKNOWLEDGMENTS

SEPTEMBER 4, 11:48PM

Christina

I'm so tired, and I have to get back to editing, so this will be short and sweet.

Jen, Cynthia, to just say I love you would not be enough, because at this point, I also hate you both quite often. I kid. In all seriousness, though, I really don't know what we did this summer…but I'm so glad we did it. These sisters stole my heart (and a lot of my time, as well as yours #ruinedmyself), but I think they needed to be here. I'm so glad for Jersey bagels, and the disco fries we didn't eat because we were busy plotting this out on the back of Cynthia's damn menu with the pen she "borrowed" from the waitress.

Waitress, I am sorry Cynthia stole your pen. I know she seemed nice, and her smile fooled you, but she took that pen and wrote some dirty things with it (#hateme). I hope you ate the rest of our fries when we finally left. We deserved that for occupying your booth for so many hours.

Casper, thank you for unknowingly giving me Joey—he wouldn't exist without you—and for your help with that chapter (you know the one). I love you. Thank you for being so *you*.

Mom, I finally wrote something happy—kind of—just like you've always wanted! I hope all the sex doesn't #ruinit. I love you, forever and then some. My next book will likely be another sad one. I'm sorry in advance.

My brothers, Tyler and Derek, I love you guys.

My brave erotic beta readers: Anna, Amanda, Diana, Rhea, Talon. Thank you. Your feedback was invaluable, and your encouragement helped get me through this more than you could ever know. So much love to you all.

Kat, for being you. My literal other half of Savage Hart. I love you and I can't wait to write with you one day. Thank you for being part of this book.

Diana, for the beautiful cover of Kitty's poetry book. You are a gem. I am so thankful we found each other. I'll come visit you in India one day.

Heathens, I live for you guys. Thank you for your undying support. I love you so much.

For everyone who was excited for this series. Everyone who shared, posted, screamed, and partook in the surprises, thank you. Thank you, thank you, thank you.

Last but not least, to Joey and Kitty. Thank you for coming to me. I'll miss you both.

ABOUT THE AUTHOR

Christina Hart is an author, editor, and animal whisperer. She has a BA in Creative Writing and English with a specialization in fiction. Her four self-published poetry collections have all become bestsellers. They can be found online, along with her six novels. Traditional publications include The Chapstick Chick (Unknown Press) and The Father They Didn't Know (Penmen Review). In her spare time, she plays with other people's books while simultaneously driving them insane in the process. She hopes you will read her other books and/or hire her to edit yours. She also hates writing bios.

ALSO BY CHRISTINA HART

Poetry

Empty Hotel Rooms Meant for Us

Letting Go Is an Acquired Taste

There Is Beauty in the Bleeding

Don't Tell Me To Be Quiet

Novels

The Rosebush Series:

Lavender and Smoke

Woods and Ash

Rose and Dust

Fresh Skin

Synthetic Love

Manufactured by Amazon.ca
Bolton, ON